TANGLED IN TWISTED IMPERFECTIONS WITH MY FIRST LOVE

MICHAEL BASKERVILLE II

D1714425

Copyright © 2023 by StarLit Publications

All rights reserved. No part of this publication may be reproduced, stored or transmitted in any form or by any means, electronic, mechanical, photocopying, recording, scanning, or otherwise without written permission from the publisher. It is illegal to copy this book, post it to a website, or distribute it by any other means without permission.

This novel is entirely a work of fiction. The names, characters and incidents portrayed in it are the work of the author's imagination. Any resemblance to actual persons, living or dead, events or localities is entirely coincidental.

Michael Baskerville II asserts the moral right to be identified as the author of this work.

Michael Baskerville II has no responsibility for the persistence or accuracy of URLs for external or third-party Internet Websites referred to in this publication and does not guarantee that any content on such Websites is, or will remain, accurate or appropriate.

Designations used by companies to distinguish their products are often claimed as trademarks. All brand names and product names used in this book and on its cover are trade names, service marks, trademarks and registered trademarks of their respective owners. The publishers and the book are not associated with any product or vendor mentioned in this book.

None of the companies referenced within the book have endorsed the book.

First edition

CONTENTS

Act One

Chapter One
The Beginning

I t was Friday afternoon, and eighteen-year-old Kofi couldn't wait until it was time to leave school. He was counting down the days to when he would be graduating. He already had most of his credits. Not only was he a jock, but he was also one of sweetest and genuine young men at Miami Central Senior High. There wasn't much he couldn't do. He was the captain of the basketball team, and he was getting college offers since he was a sophomore. Though he was getting offers from universities, basketball wasn't his aim. He had different plans for his future and his studies. He was conflicted on being able to play basketball and concentrate on his degree. All four years of high school, he was never in a meaningful relationship because he focused on school. He would bag any female he wanted when it was time to. Every chick wanted a piece of what Kofi Dixon brought to the table.

The school bell rang, and the students swarmed the hallways. Kofi grabbed his belongings and headed straight out the door. He stopped at his locker to put a few books away. He was then approached by a fellow female student. She tapped him on his left shoulder.

"Hey, Kofi." Her name was Mariah, and she was fond of Kofi for quite some time. His eyes got low in a seductive manner, and her smile was joyful yet tender when she looked at him.

"What's up, Mariah? How are you?" he asked.

There was a lot of madness in the hallways. Mariah subtly grabbed Kofi's jeans and pulled him closer to her. Kofi looked around to make sure no teachers watched or the principle.

"Damn, you're feisty. Is there something I can help you with?"

"Yes, as a matter of fact, there is. I wanted to know if you could come over this evening so you can help me study. Science isn't one of my favorite subjects, and I could use a tutor with your brains."

Mariah dragged her finger down Kofi's chest. She winked, and she was persuasive. "I mean... that's if you don't have any other plans tonight. I'm hoping you can squeeze me into your schedule."

Kofi cleared his throat. He was turned on by the way Mariah approached him and by the way she was slightly aggressive. These weren't gestures he was used to dealing with on an everyday basis.

"Let me know what time you want me to swing by. Are your parents gonna be home?"

"Nope. They'll be going out, so we can get plenty of study time in. Amongst other things."

Kofi the sound of that. "Damn. Do you care to enlighten me on those other things?"

Mariah gave off a mischievous smile, and Kofi noticed the twinkle in her eye giving off naughty vibes.

"What's your phone number so I can text you the time to come over? And you're a smart guy, so you can figure it out on your own," she replied.

Kofi wasted no time pulling his phone out of his back pocket and handed it to Mariah. "Better yet, how about *you* text *me* instead?"

Kofi slid his phone back into his pocket. "I can do that. I hope to see you later."

"Oh... you can count on it."

Kofi shook his head and sighed. *God, what did you bless me with?*

A couple moments later, Kofi's best friend, Jerrod, saw him by his locker and noticed Mariah walking away from Kofi. Kofi was mesmerized in the moment when he was watching Mariah's perfect curves strutting in the hallway with her glossy lips.

"Yo!" Kofi and Jerrod dapped each other up, happy to see each other. "Did I just see what I think I saw?" asked Jerrod playfully.

He was always attentive, but at the same time, he was the nosy best friend.

Kofi laughed. "What do you think you saw?"

"I just saw Mariah's fine ass talking to you. You seemed to be looking a lil' cozy over there before I walked up. What's going on with that?"

Before answering, Kofi shut his locker and put his back up against it and sighed. "You already know that's the plan. She wants me to fall through tonight. Her folks will be out. She dressed it up as if we're going to be studying, but obviously, she has other plans in mind that I'd be a fool to say no to, you feel me?"

While Kofi explained, Jerrod felt envious. "You

always have the juice, and it's crazy how much coochie gets thrown at you every single day that you still manage to keep up."

The friends walked down the hallway.

"You know variety is the spice of life. I worked hard these last four years, bro. We deserve to have fun, right? Work hard and play later," Kofi explained.

Jerrod was raised in Liberty Square where he spent his childhood in the Pork N Beans Projects. He was from a section where it was crime infested and violent, especially for murder. He moved once gentrification got in the mix, and his family was pushed out for renovation purposes, but he didn't let his environment dictate his legacy. The project was filled with junkies, and he risked catching a bullet at any given moment, even when he wasn't in beef. He came from the dirt and beat the odds. Him and Kofi bonded through basketball. They formed their brotherhood since the first day they met when Jerrod moved and found peace and was able to get a solid education in an environment where he didn't have to worry about catching a case or catching a shell.

"I ain't mad at you. Did you figure out what college you're gonna commit to yet?"

By this time, Kofi and jerrod were in the parking lot of the school. Busses were riding by, but both guys drove themselves to school every day.

"Most likely Miami University. I rather stay close to home. I love Miami, bro. I love the atmosphere, and I'll still have a great career. Everything I want is right here, so I can't complain," Kofi replied.

Jerrod had his mind on St. University.

"I'm proud of you. Matter fact, I should say I'm proud of *us*. We deserve our blessings, but enough about school shit right now. My brain can't function with any more school talk. I was thinking about hittin' this party tonight, but you already got your hands tied up for the night. Plenty of ladies are gonna be there, too. Bag 'em and tag 'em," Jerrod said jokingly.

"What time does it start?"

"Nine or ten tonight. It's time for some excitement."

"Okay, cool. I'll be done by then." Kofi looked at his watch. "Oh shit. I gotta go. I'll get with you later tonight."

Kofi headed home and was ready to get his weekend started. While he was on his way home, a few of his classmates saw him in traffic and waved at him. He waved back and smiled from ear to ear.

Fifteen minutes later, he was pulling into his driveway. He lived in a gated community, so he turned his music down. There were a lot of elderly folks that were in his area. He was always respectful. He walked inside his house and saw his mom in the kitchen.

"Mommy!" he yelled. "It's smells good in here. What are you making?"

"Hey, honey. Of course, I'm making your favorite."

Kofi's favorite food was Peri-Peri Chicken, a famous Ghana dish. Kofi was born in Florida and his mother, Afia, was of Ghana descent. She moved to the United States where she met Kofi's father, Lance. They married three years after. Kofi didn't have the accent, but Afia's was strong. Her English was great, though. She was hardworking, her enthusiasm was admirable, and she always gave off vibrant energy that could be contagious. She came from humbled beginnings. Her culture was a representation of unity and strength. Afia took pride in her nation and looked at being Black as a gift, and she spoon fed those qualities to Kofi. There were several times since Kofi was born that they visited Ghana. Afia made it clear that she wanted him to understand his roots and was able to learn the language. He thoroughly enjoyed visiting South Africa on occasions. Lance was Haitian. He was born in East Tampa and was raised in Olinda Projects, also where he first met Afia in the early 90s. During that time of growing up in Florida, it wasn't always glamorous. The Dixon family didn't grow up in South Beach across the bridge to embrace a flashy lifestyle. What made Florida stand out was it was a city within a city, depending on where you stayed. He could walk one to two blocks and be in another city.

"I can't wait!" yelled Kofi. He placed his bag on one of the kitchen table chairs before Afia scolded him to move it and take it upstairs because of dinner about to be served. "What time is Dad getting home?"

"I'm not sure. He's been working a lot of over-time lately." Afia seemed rather annoyed, because she couldn't see and spend time with Lance like she would've wanted to. It was stressful. "You have plans tonight?"

"Yup. Jerrod wanted me to go to a party with him tonight, but before I go to the party, I have a study session I'm going to. Is there something you need me to do?"

"No, son. A mother just doesn't want to be kept

in the dark. I just wanted to know and to make sure you're safe. You're my only child, and just because you're eighteen doesn't mean I won't worry." Afia started making the plates. "I'll just have to put your father's in the microwave for now."

Afia and Kofi ate and bonded at the dinner table.

"Are you excited for college?"

Kofi was going for his Bachelor's degree.

"With all due respect, Mom... hell yeah! Everything is falling into place. I'm grateful that you and Dad kept me on the right path with my academics. It was good idea that we prepped early as we did."

Afia agreed. "I know there was certain parts in your life to where you felt slighted on fun and missed out on things. I just always wanted the best for you, and it was in the spirit of love. Being in Ghana was hard because of the poverty. The first chance I was able to move, I had to take it. Moving to the states was the best decision I ever made."

Kofi smiled. "I'm not gonna lie, sometimes those chemistry classes used to piss me off, but I made it work."

Afia knew keeping Kofi out of trouble would've opened up a lot of career opportunities for his future, and she was right on the money. Kofi wasn't a troublemaker, and he stayed to himself. If not then he was with his inner circle. He dealt with jealousy from other peers. He was looked at as arrogant and cocky to those who never had a conversation with him but were on the outside looking in. Females were constantly around him. He had natural suave but refused to be tied down exclusively.

Kofi slept with females who even had boyfriends, but by his logic, if a female was *that* eager to pursue him by knowing they had a situation, then that was between the female and her boyfriend. He couldn't hold himself accountable for something a female initiated. Kofi didn't owe an explanation to another dude nor loyalty. His way of thinking was immature, but to him, it was what it was. Kofi didn't explain his mentality to his mom knowing she would chastise him.

"How come you don't bring over any one of your female friends?" asked Afia.

Kofi knew his house had strict rule, so it caught him off guard when Afia brought it up.

"I was afraid. I had a few I could've brought over but didn't trust how you would perceive them."

While Afia had the intuition that Kofi was sexually active since he was sixteen, no mom thought any girl was worthy of her son.

"I was young once."

"I know. I'll keep it in mind the next time I meet a nice, beautiful girl. Just please don't scare them off, and we'll be good." Kofi laughed. For his age, his maturity level was not like most, even though he was clearly a womanizer, but he couldn't help his hormones. He was good looking, charming, and was full of emotional intelligence. In middle school, he was reserved and mellow, but his state of mind changed to becoming more outgoing. Not to mention he had a hell of a glow up. He was becoming more attractive each day. While some ignored Kofi, even though they were curious due to other females wanting him, others waited to initiate the first chance they got. Though he was looked at as a player, Kofi was handsome young man. He could be egotistical if he wanted to, but that was due to being competitive in extracurricular activities. He would give the shirt off his back to others. Most of Kofi's experiences were casual, where both parties agreed, even though he broke several hearts along the way.

Kofi finished his dinner and went to take a shower. Before he got in, he got a message from Mariah that her parents were leaving at six. That bought Kofi enough time to lounge and have time to himself before also going to the house party with Jerrod. He checked his phone again after responding to Mariah, and he told her he was going to be on his way shortly.

He finished getting ready. In the midst, he heard the door open. It was Lance. Off first glance, Lance looked tired when he strolled in slowly, and he dropped his briefcase while backing up against the door.

"Dad! What's up, man?" Kofi hollered.

"What's up, son?"

"You look beat. Today must have been a mental workout for you, huh?"

"You can say that again. Today kicked my ass. How was school?"

"School was school. Nothing out of the ordinary. I'm about to head out with some friends. If it's not too late, and you're up, which I'm sure you'll probably be crashed, let's play the game so you can get washed in Madden again like last time."

"Sounds like a plan." Lance laughed tiredly. "But if not tonight, we can get busy on the game tomorrow, and I can take you across my knee."

Lance and Kofi hugged. Kofi turned around and kissed Afia on the cheek and raced out the door.

"Hi, my love," said Afia to Lance. "I left your plate in the microwave. It's nice and warm for you."

"Hi, my chocolate queen. Thank you."

Afia walked closer to Lance and leaned in for a kiss. She wrapped her arms around his waist.

"Did you already eat or were you waiting for me to come home?" he asked.

"Yes, I ate with Kofi. I didn't expect for you to be home this earlier. You should've told me."

Lance sat down at the table and undid his tie and his jacket and placed it over the chair.

"What do you want to drink?" Before Lance could answer, Afia assumed he wanted an alcoholic beverage. She poured Lance a glass of Akpeteshie, which was imported straight from Ghana.

"Thank you, baby." Lance wasted no time digging in. "Listen, I have a business trip I'm heading to. It's a great opportunity."

Afia's face became long. She didn't expect Lance to tell her that not even ten minutes into being home for the evening.

When she was in her early 20s, she started off as being a Human Resources Coordinator, and she had the luxury of being able to work from home while being pregnant with Kofi. Her job entailed recruiting, reading through people's resumes, calling potential candidates to set up interviews for direct to hire positions. It was fulfilling for a while until she wanted something better when she grew out of the company she was employed for. The main reason she left HR was because she grew tired of firing employees and struggling to fix toxic work environments. She later switched careers when she became a crime scene investigator. She had an internship, and it helped open doors for her.

She was out a lot for unexpected incidents from shootings, burglaries, fatal and non-fatal car accidents, collecting evidence with other police officers across Miami. She was also affiliated with Science Forensic Technicians. Though she had a registered licensed firearm, she never had to go to a scene armed. While she didn't make arrests or actually solve cases, the majority of her work was at the crime scene, and then the lab. She reported information to the detectives, so they could continue their investigation. Tracing evidence was her specialty. At times in her career, she used sense of humor tactics when discovering scenes to help her get through the process of potential horrifying scenes that weren't for the faint of heart.

"Monday. I'll be gone for a few days, most likely until either Wednesday or Thursday."

Afia couldn't hide her emotions because it was written all over her face. She knew what she signed up for with Lance's career.

"What's wrong?"

"Nothing, Lance. It's fine."

"No. That's not the answer, so just speak your mind. What's the problem?"

"I just miss you. There wouldn't be any other reason besides missing you. Even when you're here, it's like you're not here, and your work is more important. Even though I work tremendously, I still find time to spend with my family. You need to understand that you stressing me out isn't going to help. It's already bad enough I'm so damn fatigued. What's wrong with me just wanting to decompress? Do you understand how demanding my job can be? I don't think you do." Afia didn't want to come off insensitive or selfish, but that was how Lance was perceiving it. "I'm sorry. I just wanted to speak my mind. I can't stand the grumpy mornings. I just want to feel like I'm a priority to you."

Lance was chewing his food, and he took a drink. "I don't know what you want me to say right now, because my job is to make sacrifices, and that's exactly what I do daily," he explained. "I'm tired. I feel like I'm deprived of getting rest."

Lance's commuting was taking a toll on Afia, and she couldn't hide it. Lance had the decency to video call when he was away, but that wasn't enough for Afia to be nervous of his loyalty and wanting her bed warm at night. Being a flight attendant was hard, especially being surrounded by airline hostess that were drop dead gorgeous and gave immaculate grooming.

Afia and Lance stared at each other, agreeing to disagreeing.

"Forget I even said anything. Just enjoy your dinner. We can talk more about this later. Plus, I know you're tired." Afia removed herself and went upstairs.

Lance could tell she was still bothered by the way she stomped up the steps. Lance shook his head and continued to eat his food. Lance was a flight attendant, and that required a lot of traveling from different states and countries. He tried to be home as much as possible to avoid confrontation with his wife, but romantically, they'd been fizzling out. Lance was also preoccupied with things that didn't have anything to do with work. He would party a lot. Afia and Lance were fortunate for being together years before Lance's career became super busy. Often, Lance was gone for weeks at a time.

Afia just wanted time and stability, but marriage could crash and burn if a couple wasn't on the same page.

Kofi pulled up to Mariah's house. He parked across the street. He texted Mariah and said that he was outside. She opened the door after she got the text.

"I'm glad you could make it. I was beginning to think you were gonna stand me up." Mariah couldn't keep her eyes off Kofi.

"Now, what kind of example would I be setting if I was to stand you up?"

Mariah grabbed Kofi's hand, and they went upstairs. The two sat on the bed.

"So, what part of Chemistry do you need help with?" asked Kofi sarcastically. He knew what the deal was, but as usual, he was playing it cool.

"Ours," answered Mariah.

What Kofi respected about girls he encountered was they didn't hold back and weren't afraid to make the first move. Mariah was ready to breathe and drown in some good pipe.

Mariah kissed and nibbled on Kofi's neck. It was go-time.

"You sure you ready for this type of action?" he whispered.

"Hush," ordered Mariah. She took his shirt off and touched all around his six pack. He was in great shape because he trained a lot and was full of energy. He loved core workouts. Mariah unbuttoned his pants, and he sped up the process by unbuckling his belt. They kissed before Mariah went down. He sat at the side of bed. "Are you ready? I've been waiting for a long ass time."

"I was born ready." Kofi didn't want Mariah to talk anymore. With him being as strong as he was for his age, he held Mariah's head firmly and gagged her. He poured himself down her throat, and she took it all. He was still charged up, so he didn't need to rebuild to continue.

After Kofi climaxed, Mariah kept it going. It made him think about the psychological impact he had on girls that made them want to wrap themselves around him and do things for him in a drop of a dime. Kofi was ready to fuck Mariah. After dropping his load, Mariah was wet as a pier. He was an old soul, and as soon as he felt the stream, the song "Can You Stand the Rain" by New Edition automatically came to mind.

Kofi snatched a condom from his pants pocket and pushed Mariah's books off the bed. He turned her ass around and inserted himself. The first thing he did was look at her face. Her face validated that she was into it, and she proceeded to get punished. Each thrust felt like a snug of euphoria. It was about that time to turn up the frequency. Kofi was blessed with his package and knew how to arouse and seduced the mind before any physical was involved.

"Oh, my God!" screamed Mariah. She had two pet dogs that heard the commotion, and they were barking. They paused for a moment and started to chuckle. Kofi looked at his Apple Watch to check the time. He still had juice left in the tank. Mariah turned around fearing that he was about to leave.

"You're done already? I thought you were bringing me dick *dick*! Don't let me down!"

Kofi gave a wicked grin as he granted Mariah's request. Her desire for him was irresistible. He was too smooth.

"You're spoiled!"

They met each other at the finish line. The temperature rose in the room. Kofi was sensitive while on the brink of relief. Mariah's curvy body had the perfect arch. She looked back to see Kofi's facial expression, reassuring that she was amazing.

"I'm a different type of beast!" he yelled.

Mariah's lips twisted briefly. Kofi flexed his muscles. She was content for the rest of the night. Kofi had to get another shower before he met up with Jerrod at the party.

Chapter Two
The New Student

Monday morning at school, after homeroom let out, Kofi walked over to talk to his teacher. He wanted to ask her a few questions about schooling. Her name was Mrs. Phifer, and she was his favorite teacher. Mrs. Phifer was organizing her desk when he approached. "Mrs. Phifer, do you have a minute?"

"Of course, sweetie. What do you need?"

"I was just curious about a few things, but if you're busy, I can wait until later."

"Heaven's no. Talk to me."

Kofi snatched one of the chairs from a nearby desk and pulled it up next to Mrs. Phifer.

"I need to know other resources I can use to get involved with being a veterinarian. I know academically my marks are where they should be." Kofi's academics were top three percent in the state of Florida.

"You'll have to go to a local clinic, and I'm also sure your guidance counselor will have more answers. That's what I do know off the top of my head. Also, you could research animal shelters you could possibly volunteer at. That's your best bet. That'll show your eagerness and initiative," explained Mrs. Phifer. "And the biggest thing is, it'll help with your emotions."

"Help with my emotions how?"

"Were you ever an owner of pets?"

"I had a few cats and dogs, yeah."

"Good. How did it make you feel when those pets had to get put down? Wasn't a good feeling, was it? And I'm sure you were upset and depressed because it's like losing a family member."

Kofi agreed with Mrs. Phifer. "Of course, I was. You have a point."

"Imagine being a vet and having to be the one to tell an owner of the pet that it won't be returning home. There's going to be many cases when you're explaining how an animal can't be saved. That's conflict and won't be easy to do or handle."

Kofi had a passion for animals since a child. "I didn't look for it from that aspect."

It was a tough pill to swallow when there were people who would blame the vets for not being able to do their job to save their animal. Some things were out of their control.

"You'll have to deal with a lot of stress, so I'm hoping this is something you're ready for, and I'm not doubting you, either."

Mrs. Phifer was always brutally honest with her students. Anytime Kofi came to her, whether it be things that pertained to school or personal matters, he trusted her judgement. Kids naturally grew on teachers after seeing them for four years.

"I know I got this, and I'm motivated. I'm just ready to go in full throttle and do whatever it takes. I know it'll be a long road. The money I know will be good, but that's not the important investment," explained Kofi. He got up and gave Mrs. Phifer a hug. "Thank you so much! See... this is why I always say you're the dopest teacher to talk to! You always know what to say."

Mrs. Phifer chuckled. "That's my job, buddy. Now, get on out of here, kid, before you're late to your next class. I'll see you later."

. . .

Kofi was in a biology class. During his junior year, he took chemistry and physics. Junior year was almost the hardest year for any student and was arguably the most important year of high school. Kofi had all his assets. The current assignment was being finished up that Kofi was working on the last several weeks. He was growing a plant and was testing the temperature and light of the plant. While he was his desk, another student walked in. A female student knocked on the door, which Kofi could see by the window. It was a student he never saw before, so he assumed she was a new student. Her face looked annoyed when she walked in, but she also had a confident walk to her. The teacher got the classes attention to introduce the new student.

"Excuse me, class!" yelled the teacher unexpectedly and dramatically. "This is Liviana Washington. Please make her feel at home and introduce yourselves. Make her feel welcomed."

Liviana gave a subtle smirk as she waved and sat down at an empty desk. The teacher told her not to worry about today since it was her first day and she came in the middle of a project. She put her book bag down and sat two desks away from Kofi. Since there was down time, Kofi took it upon himself to introduce himself one on one. He made his way over in her direction, and in her peripherals, Liviana noticed Kofi coming over. The two locked eyes before any words were said. Her face was blank.

"Hi, Liviana, is it? How are you? My name is Kofi. Welcome to Miami High," he said politely.

Kofi put his hand out for a handshake. At first, Liviana was reluctant but didn't want to be too harsh on someone who was being nice.

"Hi, Kofi."

He could sense Liviana standing off, which he understood because you never could tell if someone's intentions were good off the bat, and he was a stranger. Even though she didn't say it, Liviana thought Kofi was attractive.

"Forgive me if this question sounds a little off base, and I don't mean to offend, but where are you coming from?" he asked.

"What do you mean?" she asked in confusion.

"Where are you originally from? You from a different city in Florida or from a completely different state? I'm only asking because I hear an accent when you speak."

Both were evaluating each other while looking each other in the eye.

"I'm from Atlanta. I just moved here, and as you can see, I'm not too thrilled... especially with having to move my senior year of high school. It didn't make sense to me. On another note, I'm not interested in meeting any new friends at this present moment. What's the point of doing so?"

Kofi felt bad during the conversation. "Well, shit. If you put it like that then it sounds depressing as hell, but you still have to make the best of it as cliché as it sounds. But it's our senior year. We need to have fun. If you're kind to someone then they'll be kind to you, young lady. Plus, the people you left back that I'm sure you're missing, you still keep in touch with them, right?"

Livivana gave a sly smile. "I guess you're right."

"I don't wanna take up more of your time or be invasive, but I wanted to make conversation and maybe break you out of your shell. I know it's only your first day, and maybe it's a blessing in disguise for you to meet new people and have new goals."

Liviana could've easily just curved Kofi but decided to be open to conversation with him instead. He made her comfortable. Even though Liviana was still being reserved, she still participated in class and engaged with a few classmates within a half hour span. Liviana learned fast that Kofi was popular.

Class was ending in five minutes. The teacher

was going over another project that was going to be started mid-week. That was more of a chance to engage with students. The bell rang, and everybody was leaving.

"I'll see you around?" asked Kofi. "Don't be shy. This doesn't have to be a hard transition, and don't forget my name, either. I'm Kofi. You'll be meeting hundreds of students, but I'll be the most important one," he added jokingly.

Liviana put her bookbag on. "Thank you. You sound like a guidance counselor or the principal right now, but I appreciate your words. And hopefully it doesn't take me long to get used to the new dynamics around here."

"You're welcome. It's all about adapting to your surroundings. A lot of students won't even care that you're new. The school is dope. You never know, you might fit right in. Maybe think about doing some extracurricular activities to pass the time depending on what your interests are."

"What sport do you play?" she asked.

"I play basketball, and I'm captain of the team. I've been starting since my freshman year."

Liviana was impressed. "Nice, check you out. When is your next game?"

"We play this Wednesday at home. You should

come out and show some support. The game is at seven," he responded.

"I'll have to check my busy schedule. I'll get back to you."

"That's good enough for me. I'm not gonna keep you any longer. Some of these teachers love writing students up for being late to class, but I mean, you might be able to get away with since it's your first day, and you don't know where each of your classes are. It's a big school. What's your next class by the way?" asked Kofi.

"Why? Are you going to walk me to my next class?" Liviana asked.

"I mean, if need be, I could. It doesn't sound like a bad idea now that you mention. Who wouldn't wanna walk a beautiful young lady to her classes? I might just take you up on that offer."

"I have English 12, and after that, I have a government class." Liviana was intelligent just like Kofi was, and she had the derive. She was a history guru, but where her heart lied was becoming a real estate agent. She didn't feel like scrambling through colleges her last year of school and stressing herself out. She didn't see the point unless it was about financial business related. She didn't want to put herself in unwanted debt, either. Her plan was to stay home with her mom and learn the ins and outs of agency and be a potential admin. It was the best possible outcome. She knew college would always be there in case she changed her mind in the future. Liviana's mom wasn't strict with college but wanted reassurance that she had a plan to work her way up in any field she took on. In her eyes, the biggest asset Liviana had was herself because she had the persuasion and personality to grind her way to success.

"Have fun! It was good talking to you. Make sure you learn something. That's something my mom always told me." Kofi sized Liviana up and down seductively, but it wasn't in a conquest way. Liviana, off rip, had Kofi curious because her vibe was carried different. She didn't carry herself ratchet, and she looked like a hard catch. Kofi was never truly in love before, even though he had strong feelings for girls in the past that he dated, but unconditional love was out of the question because of his relationships not lasting longer than six months.

"You have a nice day and thank you for the conversation."

Kofi was ready to tell Jerrod about Liviana right away.

"No doubt," he said as he walked away. Liviana watched him walk off.

Even though Kofi wanted to go to Miami University, The University of Florida was the only college that had Veterinarian School. He decided to make a last-minute decision to switch where he was going after graduation. He took in consideration what Mrs. Phifer said about doing volunteer work and shadowing at Vet School. He knew he would have to sacrifice sleep. The first thing he did was study his books that would help with his career post-graduation.

Kofi, Jerrod, and the rest of the basketball team were inside the locker room getting ready for practice. Since the senior year started, Kof was close to hitting one thousand points for his school. He had plenty of times to reach it and be the first player in school history to reach that milestone. Kofi was looked at like a machine. He was committed. Wednesday was one of his biggest moments. He was stoked to make his mark, an achievement that he was going to treasure for the rest of his life. It made it special that it was going to be in front of the home crowd.

"You ready for Wednesday?" asked Jerrod.

"Hell yeah! Twenty-four hours, baby!"

"You're gonna be in the rafters. How does that feel, bro?"

"Haven't processed it all the way, but I'm just ready to ball out with my team and kick them dude's asses, you feel me?" Kofi had a moment where he wasn't being modest.

"I feel you. Be hype about it. We're on the same time."

"Don't get me wrong. I'm excited, but until it happens in that moment, I'm not being overly excited if we don't win. Imagine getting that, but we lose the game. That'll piss me off. You know I never been a stat padder." It was always about the team first.

"It's about performing at a high level and being consistent and *we* excel because we're not only great at what we do, but we have tenacity and grittiness that you can't fuckin' teach!" yelled Jerrod.

"We're dedicated and competitive. We put pain in!"

The team did their daily routine of stretching to avoid injury and then followed by running laps around the gym. Kofi was always the one to light a fire under his team's asses to let them know he meant business as the captain. They worked off his energy. He constantly communicated to his team-mates and called them out on their mistakes, whether it be defensively during the game or if plays weren't run correctly during practices or a game. Jerrod was the same way, but he didn't have the same influence as Kofi. Most of the team were sophomores and freshmen, so Kofi was about to pass the torch. He loved being the positive voice. He knew when to speak less and not too fast. On and off the court, he made sure every word that was spoken was counted. He would connect with his teammates outside of basketball.

The team did a shot workout immediately after running laps. With Kofi being the captain of the team and the number one leader, he always did his shot workout the main court with Jerrod. He knew his personnel and studied them strategically. Not that he was a saint or did no wrong, but his basketball IQ level was elite. He recognized that his younger teammates were used to being in certain positions, and they would get timid in big moments. He would tell them how important preparation was, and it was the key to success, especially with crafting a skillset and not being fearful of failure.

Practice lasted for about two hours, and the team showered up after huddling up. Kofi and Jerrod didn't waste a moment to chop it up in the parking lot for at least forty-five minutes before finally taking their asses home.

"Bro, there was something I wanted to tell you earlier today." Kofi snapped his fingers, trying to remember.

"Oh yeah?"

Kofi placed his hand on Jerrod's shoulder. "Bro, check this out, man. There's this new girl in my class from Atlanta, and she's pretty as fuck! I mean... gorgeous, bro. I may be gassing her up, but she's really *that*. That *it* factor."

"What's her name?" asked Jerrod in a hype fashion.

"Liviana. Pretty ass name, too. Sexy complexion, natural pear figure body shape, curves. Smelled good. She has an aura to her that she knows she looks good, but she doesn't have to bother to even flaunt it. We talked a lot during the period. You know how we love those curves, and it makes sense with her being from Atlanta. She's built like a grown ass woman." Kofi couldn't stop expressing and describing Liviana's aesthetics and having an appreciation for it. "She looks untouched and pure. You know most of these chicks I dated or hit weren't nothing for the long term. I can't lie... off that first interaction, there was a connection between us. I'm confident in saying that."

Jerrod took a step back and snickered.

"What? What the hell you laughin' at, man?"

Jerrod kept quiet for moment. "You sound like you fell in love with her already. Sheesh, champ. That's not like you. You're talking my language, though. The love handles are essential."

"I'm just a nice guy, bro. You know this already. I can't help how my personality is. I told her about the game Wednesday, too. She said she was gonna pull up."

Jerrod shook his head. "Really? Let me guess, you gonna ask her out, too? And did you talk to Mariah?"

Kofi opened the trunk of his car to put his bag in. "Was that a crime? No such thing as too much support. And nah, it's been since Friday, but I did run into her earlier this morning but nothing major." Kofi shrugged his shoulders.

"Do tell about how good that pussy was? Details, my friend. She fiend for you that day?"

"It was fire, bro. Her ass is naughty. Shout out to her. Enough about her. I'll talk to her again when I talk to her. I'm exhausted, man. I need to mentally prepare for our game on Wednesday. I wanna study some film before I crash for the night."

"I hear you, my nigga. Yeah, go get some rest. We're counting on you. In twenty-four hours. It's your night. I'm already thinking about the celebration after."

Jerrod and Kofi embraced.

"Get to the crib safe. See you at school tomorrow."

Kofi pulled up to his house shortly after. He sat in his car for about fifteen minutes, and he drifted off a couple times. He was mentally exhausted. He also noticed his dad wasn't at the house. It'd been three days since he saw him, even though they texted a few times. The message stated he was on a business trip in Tampa Bay that he was handling and that he'd be back before the big game. Kofi wanted to make sure Lance was keeping his promise of being there. It was 8:15 when Kofi walked inside the house.

"Mom, I'm home!" hollered Kofi.

"I hear you, honey. I figured you'd be home around this time."

"Are you coming downstairs?" asked Kofi.

"Yes, I'll be down in a few minutes. I'm just getting some clothes on." Afia got dressed and walked down. "Did you talk to your father today?"

"We texted earlier before I had my practice. He

told me he was still gonna make it to the game," replied Kofi.

"Hmm."

Kofi didn't like the sound Afia made. "Why you make that noise, Mom? What's wrong? His venture must be important."

Afia grabbed a bottle of water. "No, no, no. Nothing you need to worry your handsome face about. Just adult stuff." Afia didn't want to involve her son and certain aspects of her life, especially marriage issues. She didn't want to lie to Kofi, but she didn't want to expose him to anything that may result in him resenting his father. Kofi adored his father, but Afia had it in her heart that Lance was fooling around on her. Lately, Lance's trips had been more frequent. She felt she had a right to be suspicious. To add insult to injury, when Lance was at home, the intimacy wasn't the same with Afia nor were the kisses. He was dismissive and withdrawn. The change in behavior was a dead giveaway. Afia knew Kofi was attentive to details.

"Since the weekend, Mom, I noticed you been scowling. You look moody. I know when something is off. Talk to me. I can handle it."

Afia suggested for her son to get a shower and

eat dinner before it got cold since he got in late. He wanted her to hold her, though.

After doing so, Kofi raced back down the steps and went in the living room where Afia was watching TV.

"I think your father is having an affair," she expressed. "His attitude has changed, his patience level hasn't been the same, and there's several signs I've noticed with him, and it's put me in a space." Afia didn't have proof aside from her instincts about Lance's disposition changing.

"You think so? Dad isn't that type of guy." Kofi wasn't naïve, but he was young.

Lance being her husband, Afia felt it was totally unacceptable not having his undivided attention, and the bare minimum wasn't enough, especially when she wasn't receiving that, either. She didn't want to destroy Lance's image to her son.

"Baby boy... I'm not trying to plant bugs in your ear, but you're my son, and I want to be transparent with you. This is the best way I can. I truly believe your father is cheating on me." Afia wasn't ruling out being wrong.

Kofi took a tired exhale. "If that's the case, how are you gonna handle that? Because Mom... Maybe it's not a good idea to jump to conclusions."

Afia was purposely leaving out certain details because it would be inappropriate to tell. Afia and Lance's sex life wasn't the same for a long time, especially with Afia having a high drive, and several times in the past, she would literally throw herself on her husband, and he would blow her off or be distracted, making her feel low.

While being home, all Lance's devotion was toward his work. He was preoccupied, and it was frustrating. As hard as Afia worked, she was a great multitasker and still had the ability to be devoted to her husband. She couldn't pinpoint it. She was thinking Kofi had to see for himself on how things would potentially unravel. On the outside looking in, when it came to events and traveling when they did, the Dixon family looked like perfection to people, but nobody knew what possibly happened behind closed doors.

Each day and week was becoming harder, and her overthinking was killing her internal happiness. Kofi understood the factors. Though he was a young adult, he knew exactly what infidelity was.

"You and your father have a bond, and by no means do I want to separate that at all, so I'm trying to choose my words wisely." In retrospect, she felt the conversation was out of line, and she was displaying bad parenting skills.

"I hope everything works out, and this may be a case of you seeing things that might not be there," Kofi added. "Respectfully, Mom. Not saying that your emotions don't hold any validation. Maybe Dad is just stressed or feels like he has the world on his back to take care of us." Kofi got up from the couch and kissed Afia on the cheek. "How about you just sleep on it? Tomorrow will be a better day."

While Kofi was on his way upstairs, Lance texted him and told him he was coming home tomorrow. Afia heard his phone go off.

"It's Dad. He said he'll be home tomorrow. Maybe when he gets home, you can talk. Tell him what's on your mind, Mom."

Afia raised a wise young man. "One more thing, honey, before you go to bed." Afia stopped her son on the steps.

"Yeah, Mom?"

"What does love mean to you?"

Kofi drew a breath and let it settle before answering. "I know what love is, and I like the idea of love, but at my age, I'm not in a position that I have to sacrificing myself for somebody I love like what Dad is supposed to do for you. God willing when I'm older I can provide that service to a woman who is worthy of my protection, but in the meantime, I'm gonna continue to be selfish. I don't feel I'm in a position to want to be emotionally vulnerable yet."

Kofi barely had meaningful relationships and was comfortable with the single life and the girls he dealt with that didn't mind being seduced by him and vice versa.

"Interesting perspective. On the flipside, when you fall in love, make sure you keep your integrity and stay committed. Practice the art of being stable. Be loyal like the woman should be to you. I'm not against you having fun. You're a good kid. Everything changes once you place your heart on the table."

Chapter Three
Romantic Liars

I t was Tuesday morning, and Lance was unpacking his bags from his business trip. He talked to a few neighbors in the complex before entering the home. Afia left for work about thirty minutes before he came in. He was home by himself since Kofi was at school. It gave him time to relax all day and decompress. He opened some mail that sat on the kitchen table, did some cleaning, and worked out in the weight room he put together outside.

After working out and washing up, he looked at his phone, and he had a couple of missed messages and other notifications from the last hour. It was from a mistress he went away and met up with on his business trip, proving that Afia was correct. Lance was keeping this going for several months and keeping up the façade that he was happily married to Afia. It was clear that Lance didn't care about breaking his wedding vows and didn't honor his woman like he was supposed to. He replied to the missed messages saying he missed her and couldn't wait to see her again.

Lance was consistently annoyed with Afia. There were times at night he would be lying down, and he would reflect on how long his affair was going on. He just wanted to feel again, even if that meant being with another woman from time to time. The woman he was sleeping with was also married. Neither one of them had regrets, and if they did at any moment, then it was quickly diminished. Lance had chemistry with the woman, along with lust in their hearts to the point that acting on the temptation was an easy decision. The woman would tell Lance about her husband and things that went on inside the house, which was the ultimate violation. Lance would have his opinions, and even went as far as telling the mistress why he was a better fit for her, which was totally disrespectful. They were too far gone from respecting boundaries, and they were risking World War III.

Wednesday evening, Kofi had to rush back home to get his mouth guard for his game. When he got home, he was greeted by his parents.

"Game day!" he hollered.

"You know it!" replied Lance with enthusiasm.

The game was starting in two hours. Kofi raced up the steps. "I wanna get some shots up and then watch junior varsity play."

"I'll take you back, so you don't have to drive home after," Lance suggested.

"That works for me!"

Afia was in the kitchen. "Baby, you also forgot this." Afia handed Kofi his Gatorade bottle.

"Thanks, Mom! Appreciate you! You guys ready to go?"

"I'll meet you guys at the gym," said Afia. "I promise I won't be late."

Lance gave Afia a kiss.

"Sounds good. See at the game, Mom!"

Afia waved as Lance and Kofi pulled off. Afia walked back in the house and went upstairs. Lance's

Chromebook was sitting on his office desk. She flipped it up. Surprisingly, Lance didn't have a password on it. She sat down, and the first thing she did was check his history. Her leg shook from anxiety of what she might see. She immediately went to Google Maps and saw the places Lance went, which contradicted his business trip angle. She saw intimate pictures and websites in the history box of escorts. This justified her suspicion.

While Afia was scrolling through the information, she heard the doorbell ring multiple times. Afia was puzzled, so she stood up and looked out of the window. She saw a white Mazda CX-5 parked outside in her driveway. She walked down the steps and answered the door. It was a man standing there, and he looked pissed off.

"Um... can I help you, sir?" The man looked behind Afia and was sort of scoping the house to see who was in there. His eyes were tightened. They were darkened as if he didn't get much sleep and was stressed. She snapped her fingers because he was in a daze sense. "Sir, may I help you with something? Can I ask who you are?"

"Is this where Lance lives?" the man asked.

"Is there a reason you're asking?" Afia was

confused and was getting nervous, because the random man looked deeply bothered.

"And are you his wife?"

Afia didn't know if she should say another word.

"Yes," she replied with a concerned tone.

The man put his head down before bringing it back up. "So, you're the wife on the nigga who's been fuckin' my wife?" he screamed with authority. The vein in his forehead popped out and throbbed.

Afia had her hand on the door. "Wait, what? Excuse me?"

Afia was trying to process the words that came from the man's mouth.

"You heard what I said loud and clear. And he's been fuckin' my wife for quite some time now. By the way, my name is Malcolm. I work with your husband. I have for a couple years. He's been having an affair with my wife. By your facial expression, I can tell you may have had an idea that your man hasn't been living right. I'm just here to give you confirmation on something you most likely had a hunch about."

Malcolm analyzed Afia's body language and read her right away. Especially by the way her eyes danced around when he told her about his wife and Lance. Afia immediately felt emotionally fractured.

Her heart dropped to her feet, and her throat closed up.

"How long has this been going on?"

"About six to seven months. When I put the puzzle together that she was cheating, I approached the situation before, and I told her funky ass that she needed to end the affair right away, but apparently not, because... well, I'm standing on your doorstep. And quite frankly, ma'am, the only reason I haven't beat the dog shit out of your husband and he's not sleeping with the angels is because I love my career, and I love the shit out of my children. My kids are the most important to me. I'm not partaking in spending my life in prison, even though the idea floated around in my head plenty of times. What I did was call him about it initially and had a man to man conversation with him and told him to leave my wife the fuck alone. Clearly, he doesn't give a fuck about his reputation. The funny thing is I let him know if it continued I would tell you. He must have took my ass for a joke so now the cat is out the bag."

Afia was boiling.

"Stupid ass cheating fuckin' bastard!" Afia roared. Her nose flared, and her eyes squinted. While screaming out a bunch of adjectives from

Malcolm divulging the information about the affair, she was totally locked into misery. It was hard to stay composed. Not only did she find evidence of cheating on Lance's laptop, but the proof walked right on her porch. She tried to maintain herself before heading to Kofi's game in an hour.

"Quite a bomb that I dropped on you, huh?" Malcolm was loving it. He stood there while watching her call Lance every name under the sun. She had to figure out how to confront Lance. "And to think I've been living my vows with this piece of shit." This was total satisfaction to Malcolm.

"What is your wife's name?"

"Like they say, secrets have a way of revealing themselves. Sometimes, you don't even have to do anything. Her name is Diana, and you mean soon to be ex-wife," Malcolm corrected.

"Right..." said Afia.

"You can do what you want with those particulars. Apologies for bombarding like this, but I'm tired of this bullshit. They want to be together or think they can do whatever they want and get away with it, they can have each other. I was done taking the high road. Tell him I'll see him soon." Malcolm walked off the porch and drove off.

Afia slammed her door. She had to get ready for

the game. Malcolm rightfully so had a Vvndetta against Lance. Afia was in the same boat as Malcolm. The affairs they found about with their spouses had lies throughout, so even when Afia thought about how she was going to talk about the allegations, she had to prepare herself for seeds of doubt and more lies with a sprinkle of manipulation tactics as well.

The game was starting soon. She got her purse and hauled ass out the door. Even with the opportunity and privilege Lance had at work, he didn't care about crossing the line for spicy adventures.

The basketball team was in the locker room, and they were pumped up for this game. The coach was going over the last minute game plans before going out on the court to warm up. He had to make sure his team was on point with the instructions he was giving so there weren't any discrepancies. A team had to be disciplined at all times, or the team would be dysfunctional and toxic. The team could hear the crowd from inside the gym.

"Okay, guys. It's show time!" yelled the coach.

The team clapped and yelled.

"Bring it in, guys!" hollered Kofi. "This is our house, and we gotta fight for four quarters! We can't let our foot off the gas. *We* dictate the tempo of this game. *We* play with intensity, but most importantly... we play together." When Kofi spoke. The team gained more of an adrenaline rush and excitement. "Let's get out here and win this damn game!"

"Let's go!" screamed the team in unison.

They ran out and while the cheerleaders screamed, and the crowed scream and clapped. They did their layup lines for ten minutes and then shot around until it was time for tip off. There was music playing in the background throughout the gym, but Kofi went inside his gym bag and grabbed his headphones to lock in. He walked over to Lance, and they did their special handshake. From afar, Kofi noticed that Liviana was walking in. As she paved her way inside the gym, she looked around and spotted Kofi. She waved, and he jogged over to her.

"Hey, I'm glad you made it!"

"Yeah, I wasn't busy after school, so I figured why not catch a good basketball game. Go off tonight."

"You got it!" he replied.

Liviana made her way to find a spot on the bleachers to watch the game. With so many students in the bleachers, she was lucky to get a spot to sit.

It was down to the five minute mark before the game. Kofi was hype and was focused. The announcer said the names of the starting lineup. Kofi and Jerrod had their pre-game ritual where they stabilized and prepared themselves for the game. Getting nervous before games was natural. Jerrod walked up to Kofi while he wiped the bottom of his sneakers for traction. "You got this, my nigga. Remember, you're the leader. Lead the way and take this home."

Kofi nodded. "Absolutely. It's time to hold the territory down."

The team huddled up before the first quarter started. Kofi looked over to see where Afia was at, and she was just coming in. She blew Kofi a kiss and gave him thumbs up. She saw where Lance was sitting at and sat right next him, even though she didn't want to. A plethora of students were hollering for the team. The student section was filled with upperclassman, and several girls hollered Kofi's name. It was finally tip off time.

. . .

The game was tight. Both teams were going back and forth with the score. With this game, Kofi's main concern was getting his teammates involved in almost every possession. He had more assists than he had points at the time. He had fifteen assists, five steals, and thirteen points. Kofi's points for all his high school career was sitting at nine hundred and eighty, which meant he dominated in the fourth quarter. He wasn't being selfish, but when Kofi got into a certain bag offensively, he was unstoppable, and even just trying to contain him defensively was a hard task to maintain. He was strong as hell. He was finishing layups fast. The speed was undeniable. He was great at shielding the ball from a defender. Kofi had perfect body control. While Kofi wasn't scoring, he was making countless entry passes to his teammates. Kofi stood at six foot four, and he was only a freshman.

Down the stretch, Kofi scored ten more points. He was dunking left and right, sacrificing his body from diving on the floor to get loose balls.

"Get the ball, baby!" screamed Afia from the stands.

Lance kept standing up.

"My boy! Let's go!"

There were times Lance stood up. He was

receiving dirty looks from Afia but didn't notice it. She had to tell herself to cut it out because it wasn't the time. She shook it off momentarily.

One of Kofi's teammates grabbed a rebound and passed it to Kofi. He was in a triple threat position. He dribbled and created separation so the defender couldn't get the ball or block his shot. Kofi was foul but still made the basket and headed to the free throw line. He was about to complete a four point play. When it was necessary, Kofi could be a one man wrecking crew. He had the mamba mentality like the late great Kobe Bryant. The team was down by one point with thirty seconds on the clock. The coach drew up a play to get the ball to Kofi. They had a feeling that the opposing team would know who the ball was going to. The team had it in their minds that they weren't gonna be stopped, and the big play they worked on countless times was gonna work. They were ready for the crowd to roar.

Kofi grabbed the ball in bounds. He dribbled until he had enough space for a good shot but needed a screen. Jerrod set a pick on Kofi's defender. He drove to the basket for a layup, but the paint was too clogged up. Kofi passed to Jerrod at the three-point line. Jerrod's defender played great recovery defense. He gave it back to Kofi on a give-n-go. Kofi was wide open in the corner. He caught the ball and shot it. It was nothing but net. He was clutch! He scored his one thousand points on a buzzer beater! The student section erupted!

Kofi jumped up and down. "Hell yeah! Hell Yeah!" he screamed while swinging his fists in the air.

Lance jumped up in joy and dramatically ran laps around the court. The students swarmed the court instantly. The away team dropped their heads down in defeat due to Kofi's greatness and especially great coaching. The team shook hands with them to display good sportsmanship.

"Good game, fellas."

The fact that this was a rivalry game made the victory even sweeter. Lance and Afia let Kofi have his moment before they embraced him. A lot of girls were taking pictures with him and making social media posts. Kofi felt like a celebrity. After taking pictures, he hugged his coach. Liviana was still in the stands, and she was happy she made it to such a game of that magnitude. She couldn't wait to run into him tomorrow morning to congratulate him. Kofi was preoccupied and was overwhelmed with love. Lance and Afia walked up to Kofi. Afia kept kissing his face. He got the game ball, and he cried as he dropped on one knee.

After coming home from the game, Afia kept her poker face on and was waiting until Kofi was upstairs before talking to Lance. His game was phenomenal, and she didn't want to take away his glory. Kofi and Lance were jumping around in joy as they got out of the car. She clapped her hands when she got out of the car. "My baby, I'm so proud of you."

"Thank you, Mom!" he yelled. He was still charged all the way up. It was an amazing feeling for him to fulfill his expectations. He lived this moment. The closer Afia was getting to the house and looking at Lance acting like everything was peachy, the more she got the feeling of thick syrup running through her veins. Kofi quickly turned around and hugged Afia again. He was sweaty. "We did it, Mom!"

"No, baby, *you* did it." She looked at Lance once more with a smug face. She couldn't hold it in any longer, but she shifted over to Kofi to let him know she needed to talk to his father in private. "Head upstairs, baby, and get showered up."

Lance cleared his throat. "Man... hell of a game, wasn't it?"

"Yeah, it was." Afia placed her purse on the on the kitchen table. She didn't give Lance any eye contact.

"What's the problem?" he asked because it looked like Afia was pouting. She was putting the dishes away, and then she stopped abruptly.

"I thought when we got married we became responsible for each other's existence. You know... like being each other's better half."

Lance's eyes squinted in confusion since Afia was being cryptic. "What is this about exactly? Why are you saying this?"

"I don't believe you've been telling the truth about your whereabouts. I think you've been lying to me. I sacrifice a lot of you and would've done anything for you in the drop of a dime. You're not being truthful with me."

Lance became annoyed. "What I don't under- stand is that I have to always hear the same bullshit with you over and over, Afia! When does this shit stop with you? Why do I feel like this marriage is based off interrogations all the time? This shit is unbelievable."

Afia felt like smacking the bullshit out of Lance. "And why every time I bring something to your attention, you decide to start an argument, Lance? I'm expressing a problem I have with you. I've felt distance between us and that your mind has been wandering off into other places that it shouldn't be in."

Lance put his hands on his hip and scoffed. "Afia, you told me you'd be understanding about my career. We've been married for almost ten years, and you knew what this was."

Afia noticed he was flipping the script. "It doesn't feel like I have a lover at home. I feel like it's just convenient, and you're my roommate. You go to sleep right away. I get it when it comes to exhaustion... but damn, when do my needs get met? There's a division somewhere," Afia explained. She put her hands together in frustration when she saw Lance roll his eyes trying to avoid the conversation.

"Seems like we're doing each other a disservice at this point. I love you, and I respect you, but we're being unfair to each other, clearly. You're not happy. And I'm trying."

Afia's heart was beating faster. "Are you cheating on me?"

"What the fuck did you just ask me?"

"You heard exactly what the fuck I just asked you. Are you having an affair on me?" It instantly became a battle stare between Afia and Lance. "Does a cat have your tongue? And the longer it takes you to answer me means there's more of an indication I'm not wrong for my feelings. It should be a yes or no question, and I'll apologize for being out of line."

"This is what you're pulling now? I haven't been in the house that long, and you bringing bullshit to my attention."

Lance turned into a garbage person, and Afia could sense that he was stalling. "Your reverse psychology isn't going to work on me, and it's insulting. Knock it off." Afia already had the evidence, and there was no way Lance could get around it without blatantly lying to her face.

"You have the answers, don't you? So, let's talk about it."

Afia's jaws locked, and she stormed upstairs to the bedroom.

"Where are you going?"

Afia grabbed Lance's Chromebook and showed

the pictures she saw and showed him the history on this Chromebook.

"Escorts? Are you paying for sex with other women now? Are you going to say something, or do you choose to stay silent like a coward?"

"What do you want me to say?"

Afia couldn't believe the audacity Lance had. Afia was strong, and as much as she was hurting inside, she didn't have self-esteem issues.

"Who is Diana?" Lance's facial expression changed as soon as Afia name dropped Malcolm's wife. "Sleeping with another man's wife is what you decide to do? And get this, do you know that after you left for the game, he came here to share your great news that you're fuckin' her? You were warned. And you deserve whatever the fuck happens to you. I hope he kicks your ass. This marriage is a failure."

Lance folded his arms.

"I'm a man." Lance gave Afia the lamest excuse, making Afia's jaw drop.

"So, you think you can just do what you want?" asked Afia. "You're a cocky bastard. But how about this... how about you be single." Afia was fired all the way up. "Just know that one man's problem is another man's opportunity. You would really want to risk your relationship and our health for some bitch that doesn't mean a goddamn thing to you?" She was furious.

Instead of celebrating Kofi's victory, they totally made the rest of the night about them. Kofi finished washing, he got settled but heard the commotion and paced in confusion. He was getting calls and texts of countless congratulations on social media but didn't have his phone in hand. He could hear the muffled argumentation going on and checked on his parents.

"People never seize to amaze you, but what happened today was fate," said Afia. "For a long time now, you no longer were my husband I fell in love with, and now you're a villain. You're nothing more in my eyes."

"Mom? Dad? Why are you fighting?" Kofi already had an idea from the previous conversation he had with his mother.

Afia rubbed her forehead and didn't know what to say.

"Hey, son. We're just conversing, that's all," said Lance to try cut the tension in the living room.

"Dad, stop. I'm too old for that. I'm not a baby."

Afia turned to Kofi. "Remember what we spoke about the other day?"

"Yeah."

"Your father is a coward. He's the MVP," Afia was blunt. "Looks like he's been distracted by other endeavors. Listen, son. This isn't what I wanted and forgive me for the timing of this. I think it's time for me and your father to leave each other alone. I'm not telling you this to choose between me or him or change the way you feel about anything, but I'm clearly not where he wants to be."

Lance felt Kofi looking at him.

"Is this true, Dad?"

"You felt that was appropriate to tell him?" All Lance could do was tell Kofi that it was complicated for him to understand. After a hard game, this was the last thing he expected to be hearing about. He was already physically exhausted.

"Complicated how?" Lance struggled to find the words to say.

"Go head, Lance. Tell our son why you venture out to other places. Tell him about your business trips you claim to be on." Afia was aggravated. The drama could have been avoided, and so could her pain. Kofi was disturbed, and Afia was acting in a distasteful manner. Lance refused to act out of character in front of his son and had a better idea.

"I know you have school in the morning, but

come with me," Lance ordered. He wanted to have a man to young man conversation. Afia's eyes darkened as she breathed heavier. Her lips were compressed, and she stormed out of the living room. Kofi was thinking that his dad was evidently going to be sleeping downstairs. "I'm not keeping you out late, but let's go for a ride."

Kofi braced himself.

After they had been on the road for a few minutes, Lance spoke. "I want you to listen to me from father to son, and you have to listen before you start asking questions. What did I always tell you?"

"In order to be a good talker you have to be a better listener," answered Kofi.

"Very good. Now, I'm going to be completely transparent with you. Me and your mother have grown apart, and I chose to react in ways that were fucked up. It's reprehensible, and I'm indeed aware of that. By no means will there be any pressure on choosing sides like your mom said. I'm not bad mouthing your mother, either, but what I disagree on is her clearly pointing out my flaws or alluding to bad traits I have romantically to you." Afia wasn't taking in account that while she spewed out things about Lance and negative parts of their marriage, she was at the same time pointing out genetic flaws inside of Kofi. "I fucked up a lot, but that doesn't define who I am as your father, which is the most important job of mine." Lance lost himself but was holding himself accountable and wasn't going to play victim when Afia was the victim in the situation.

"What is it about other women?"

"Us as men are risking temptation every day, son. Some will be stronger than others. You can't be naïve or delusional to think when it's your time to be in a meaningful relationship there won't be other women trying to see what's going on with you. It's just how it is," explained Lance. "You're my son, and you're half of my genes. Do you understand me?"

Kofi looked at Lance while processing. Hearing his parents argue and finding out that Lance was having an affair with multiple women, even though only one came to the forefront, was a lot. Lance was choosing excitement over having stability, even though he didn't love Afia any less.

"I get it."

Lance refused to be politically correct with his son. Kofi knew even at his age that he loved variety when it came to girls, and he wouldn't know what type of reality he'd have with being a one-woman man when the time was right. Lance wanted Kofi to understand that everybody was human, and all people practiced the propensity of hypocrisy.

"Can you and Mom get through this? Like... how long have y'all been in this rut? I didn't even notice this."

"Because you weren't supposed to be. We are supposed to protect you from shit like this. You're our child. Marital issues aren't your focus. Your focus is school. That's it. And obviously staying out of trouble like you've been doing." Lance was straight forward and told Kofi that the romance between him and his wife was gone for months. The passion that Kofi's parents once shared became weak.

"Are you gonna get a divorce?"

"I'm not sure. It could be a possibility."

That wasn't the answer that Kofi wanted to hear. "Is it a possibility you can love more than one person? I mean, that's if you do love this other woman. I'm just trying to understand what this exactly is."

Lance was unsure how to respond. "I do believe it's possible to love more than one woman and vice versa." Lance had a decision to make. He could either stay in a toxic environment or could find peace to make up with Afia. At least, if she was up to it. If that was the case, he would have a lot of making up to do. The relationship suffered.

"Why does this feel like a hopeless situation? I don't remember seeing Mom that angry before. I've seen disagreements, but this hit different." Kofi was showed he was visibly upset. "To be real, maybe this is a wake up for me and that marriage life isn't for me. My bad for saying that, Dad, but if this is what I have to look forward to, then I'd rather not," explained Kofi.

"You hungry?" asked Lance to change the subject.

"Yeah, I could eat. I worked up an appetite."

They stopped at a close fast food restaurant, ordered their food, and continued to talk. Lance was under some pressure to either continue or just end his romantic and sexual relationship with Diana.

"I have a lot of girls at school, and even that can be exhausting," Kofi said. "Are you able to separate sexual from emotional?"

"I'll just say that not everything is black and white. Some shit has to be seen with a grey area. My will was tested, and I knew exactly what the hell I was doing. I can't control everything, son. One day, you'll see what I mean. You're going to be left with a lot of choices that won't be mutually exclusive."

"I guess I'll cross the bridge when I get there. It'll be awkward in the house with you and Mom. I'm not looking forward to that."

Lance got silent. "Any person you encounter will have different personalities, Kofi. You may dive into a situation where you feel you need a gap to be filled, and someone you have your eye on may help free you. Think about when you go to sleep tonight. Come on, let's head back home."

Chapter Four
Preparing for The Future

Kofi was the talk of the school the following day. He kept yawning throughout the day. He got a standing ovation throughout the hallways. Students clapped and whistled.

"Kofi, can I get a picture with you, please?" asked a fellow female student.

"Sure, why not?" he replied.

Kofi was being treated like he was entering the NBA draft. He went to his locker, and there were sticky notes on the front of his locker with phone numbers attached. There were seven different numbers. Kofi shook his head. He wasn't in the best mood, due to last night, but he was trying to keep himself upbeat because he made history.

• • •

In the afternoon, he walked inside of a study hall room, and he saw Liviana was in there.

"Well, well, well. I didn't expect to run into here. It was nice to see you at the game last night. Thank you for the support. It's appreciated, for real." Kofi sat his bag down.

"You're welcome. The game was intense. You did an amazing job. How does it feel to be the most popular and loved person in the whole school?"

"What makes you think I'm the most popular and loved?" Kofi jokingly acted like he didn't know he was. "Feels good, but I don't let it get to my head. Last night was lit, though. It's surreal, but I'm just counting my blessings and staying humble at all times."

"That's a good way to look at it," Liviana replied. "I also seen your fan club, too."

At first, Kofi didn't know what Liviana was referring to. "What fan club?"

Liviana showed disdain. "I walked by your locker and saw your love notes." Kofi thought Liviana was being passive aggressive in the moment. "I bet they fall right into your little honey trap. I'm sure of it."

"Why do you care? You seem to have it all figured out. Is that bad if I have a fan club? Maybe I can't help it." Kofi sneered, and Liviana did the same in return.

"Nope, and not at all, even though you're probably shallow and have no sincerity."

Kofi didn't know whether Liviana was being sarcastic or patronizing. He couldn't read her. "Interesting. Do you think I have these selfish motives 24/7 and have all these girls sulking in misery?"

Liviana shrugged her shoulders. "You said it. Not me."

She had a point about some of the girls that Kofi had relationship with, but he wasn't gonna admit to her. Several girls in the past wasted no time opening and revealing themselves to Kofi outside of physical interaction. Kofi was thinking about his dad's situation and tried to put himself in his shoes. He was thinking about if his actions were embedded inside. A father's son tries to impress and observe their father.

Kofi kept a dominant grin on his face and controlled the conversation. "You're coming off kind of judgmental, don't you think? Or you're going off your personal experiences with guys that may have treated you wrong. Are you passing that energy off to me? Maybe somebody promised you the world and broke that promise."

Kofi and Liviana's conversation was quiet since they were in study hall, but Kofi's voice rose, and he was aggressive. He felt he hit below the belt possibly, which was unwarranted.

"Shit... I'm sorry," he said quickly. "I got some shit on my mind."

Liviana didn't take it personal. "It's fine, you're good. Like what? If you feel like talking about it, then we can, but it's totally up to you."

"No offense, but not right now," Kofi said respectfully.

"Are you sure?" Kofi didn't feel like bothering Liviana with nonsense. "I'm invading your privacy right now and getting in the way of your study hall time."

"Oh... *Now* you're worried about my study hall time? We're already past that point already, shawty." Kofi changed the subject. "What are you studying?"

"I'm just finishing up a few assignments from a couple different classes. Study hall is where you can get a peace of mind. A lot can go on in these eight hours with other students. I have some government class assignments that I need to do. I like to stay ahead of the game. You know how that is."

"Too well I do," Kofi said. "What are your plans after school?"

"I don't have anything planned. My life is boring."

"Good. How about we grab a bite to eat so I can show you some good ass Miami food around these parts." Liviana showed interest, but Kofi almost forgot he had basketball practice. "Matter fact, instead of today, how about tomorrow? I just remembered I have prior engagements."

Liviana told Kofi that she would be free whenever. "I'm to myself, but I do need to work on being better with going out more."

"We'll fix that right away. That face is too pretty to not show it off and be one with the world. Love life and eat great food. That'll put you in the best mood possible. I'll give you a timeframe, and you can catch a vibe with me." Kofi used his charm and persuasion, and it worked marvelously.

"What do you have in mind for food? I better be impressed because Atlanta is unmatched."

"I can only take your word for it. How about this? I think we should exchange numbers, and I'll let you know a time I can pick you up," he suggested with confidence and suave.

"Why do you need my number to let me know when you can tell me right now?" Liviana's face gave off a subtle twitch.

"I can answer that with ease. Because since the first time we met in class your first day and right at this moment, I'm someone you're interested in talking to." Kofi was simply being himself, and he didn't have to use corny techniques to persuade a girl or bully her to give him her number. "Furthermore, I'm just being friendly. You can appreciate that."

Liviana put her pencil down and directly looked at Kofi, even when she tried to resist small attachment when looking in his eyes. "What if I tell you I'm not comfortable with you having it? Will your offer still stand, or will you choose not to talk to me?"

Though it was childish, Liviana was testing Kofi.

"Then you simply say no," he responded. "No harm. No foul. I'm not a creep. You don't owe me a damn thing, and I would still wanna take you out." Kofi remained smooth and polite. "Your truth works for you, and I can't do anything but respect it. I have no tricks or gameplays up my sleeve."

A chortle escaped Liviana. "Hmm." She was impressed by Kofi's maturity and that he didn't resort to being clever to score a phone number. "I see. I see."

The teachers in school were surprisingly lenient on students having their phones out. As long as they didn't go overboard and respected the teaching hours.

"Hand me your phone," Liviana ordered in which Kofi complied.

She typed her number in, and Kofi saved it. "I'm calling you right now so you can have mine. Please use it whenever. If there's spots in the area you're unfamiliar with around here, then let me know, and I can be your personal tour guide." Liviana's phone was on silent when Kofi called it. "I'll send you a selfie of me, and then you can add it to the contact. Make my contact special."

Liviana blushed softly. "Why are you so full of yourself? You're lucky you're sweet. I can admit it." Liviana entertained Kofi but wasn't all the way sold yet, and she didn't want to be another statistic to Kofi. In a matter of forty-eight hours, she wasn't oblivious to Kofi's clout and star power in the school.

. . .

Kofi had a half day at school. He found a veterinarian clinic program that was in need of volunteer to help with Animal Clinics. He walked inside the building.

"Hello, what can I help you with?" asked the receptionist at the desk.

"Hello, good morning. I researched about this place online. I'm a senior in high school, and I was inquiring about possibly observing on animal surgeries."

The receptionist called the doctor to come talk with Kofi. "One moment, please."

"Okay."

Kofi waited for about fifteen minutes. At the time, one of the doctors was with a family who was putting their dog down. Kofi could hear the screams and cries in one of the rooms. He felt horrible and sat down until he spoke with the doctor. The family walked by as they were leaving. It was a mess. The doctor walked to the front of the lobby while putting the stethoscope on her neck. The receptionist explained why he was here.

"Good morning." The Nurse's name was Kelly Hall.

"Good morning, ma'am. My name is Kofi Dixon, and my goal is to be a veterinarian. Before you say anything, I want you to know I'm dedicated, and I would love to get the opportunity to be under your wing and show me the levels of what you do." Kofi had a mystifying aura to him. "I'm coming straight from high school. I had a half day today, so I have plenty of time. I don't mind getting my hands dirty nor do I need to see the *fun* side of being a vet. Let me have it. I'm your guy. I have no criminal background, either."

"Do you mind cleaning cages and watching and feeding animals?" asked Kelly.

"No, ma'am. Not at all."

"How old are you?"

"I'm eighteen, and by the way, do my high school marks have anything to do with my education for vet schooling?"

"That's a good question, and no, they don't. Anybody can go to an undergrad program that will lead you to the next destination for schooling," Kelly answered. "With that being said, are you *sure* you don't mind smelling feces, pee, or any other fluids? I want to make sure you're fully aware. I'm not gonna sugarcoat that there's a lot of gross shit you need to take in account. I'm not gonna romanticize it. I play no games. This is your goal for your career?"

"It absolutely is."

"You know, Kofi, I've seen a lot of young adults and high schoolers that wanted an opportunity that finished programs and realized later that being in this field wasn't truly for them. To be blunt, I do not feel like having my time wasted. My time is valuable."

"I have time."

"When can you do orientation and training?" asked Kelly.

"Is it available on the weekends?"

"Yes, it is."

"Mark me down, and excuse my language, Nurse Hall, I don't give a damn about being paid. I know the behaviors of animals. I want the experience. That's what I care about."

Kelly saw the ambition and seriousness in Kofi's eyes. She wanted him to go back to his school to find out if his school allowed compensation in exchange for school credit. She also told him he would have to fill out a volunteer form so all his hours would be recorded from the day he started until the day he graduated.

"I've done plenty of research. I read up about the neglecting of animals and the welfare. I'm committed. I know I'm a little behind since I'm a senior, but my marks back up my case. I'm all about the grind. If I have structure, I won't let you down."

Kelly looked at the receptionist. "We'll give it a try and see how you work out."

Kofi kept his chin up high to show his professionalism. "Yes, ma'am. I will be in touch."

Chapter Five
Empty Smiles

Kofi called Jerrod to meet up to get a shot workout at a local gym to stay sharp and in shape. Jerrod was getting his car back next week, so Kofi had to pick him up. When they arrived at the gym, Jerrod noticed Kofi didn't say much in the car. It was a silent drive there, which made Jerrod feel awkward. He figured he was just focused on getting shots up to maximize the time in the gym, or he was just bothered. "You good, man?"

"Yeah, I'm good. Why you asking me that?" asked Kofi.

Jerrod was just getting one word answers. Jerrod picked up Kofi's last rebound and gave him a perfect chest pass for him to sink his next shot. "Because you're barely talking."

Kofi's face still remained a grimace. The last couple weeks, Kofi's mood swings were on and off.

"Nigga... I'm fine, bro. Can we just get back to our shot workout?" Kofi built a wall up to not talk about his parent's divorce. He squeezed his eyes shut and bounced the ball hard on the floor before shooting. He missed a couple of shots in a row. He missed again, and it pissed him off. "Come on, bitch! Get in the hoop!"

Jerrod still wanted Kofi to be direct with him on why his emotions were where they were at. "Listen, basketball can wait, bro. I don't mean to be pushy, but you're on the edge, and it shows."

Kofi placed the ball down and walked closer to Jerrod. "Yo, J. Are you my friend?"

"You already know," he replied quickly.

"Okay, then if you're my friend you'll respect my wishes when I say to drop the shit. Now, come on. Let's finish strong. It's your turn."

"Wait, wait." Jerrod stopped Kofi and gave the ball back. "You missed mad shots. What's the cardinal rule in basketball that we live by?"

Kofi completely forgot that he never stopped on missed shots. "Shit, you're right. Way to keep me on my toes."

"That's why I'm here."

The friends fist pumped. Kofi sunk his next couple shot and passed the ball back to Jerrod. "Now it's your turn."

After the shot workout around the different parts on the perimeter of the court, they ended the session with playing one on one. Even though they were friends, they were always enemies on the court and treated each other as oppositions and didn't hold back. They played hard and physical. The one on one matchup got chippy between trading baskets. The game was going to thirteen. Kofi was lacking focus. Jerrod was winning, and the score was ten to five.

"I'm bustin' your ass right now! Come on! Play some defense!"

Both were drenched in sweat. Jerrod scored again.

"You can't stop me!" he screamed.

Kofi snarled and played tighter defense on Jerrod. Kofi was hand checking Jerrod. He smacked Kofi's hand away.

"Get off me!" Jerrod hit Kofi with a good move that made him bite the bait on defense. When Kofi tried to recover to prevent Jerrod from scoring, he took a cheap shot route by pushing to where he could've potentially injured him.

"Ugh" grunted Jerrod. "What the fuck is your problem, nigga?" His eyes were bulged out.

"What?" replied Kofi with his arms out. "What you tryna do?"

Kofi pushed Jerrod, and Jerrod pushed him back. The two got into a grappling match, and Jerrod put Kofi in a headlock.

"Get the fuck off me, yo!"

With both of them sweating and stinking, Kofi's nostrils flared up because of how Jerrod had him locked up. His face was near his armpits, which he took offense to. His muscles tightened up on his face.

"Nah, nigga. Not until your ass calms the hell down. You lost your mind right now."

Kofi gave Jerrod a couple of body shots. Both Kofi and Jerrod's teeth were gritted tightly. Kofi was like a hurting animal waiting to attack.

"You ready to talk now?" They calmed down and sat in the middle of the court while catching their breath. "Now that we got that dumb shit out of the way, what's troubling you, man?"

"I'm scared."

"Scared of what?"

"I think my parents are gonna divorce, and it's been high key eating at me, but I can't lie and say I didn't see the signs already before it go to the point it's at now."

Jerrod was surprised. "Wow, that was unexpected. Mr. Lance and Mrs. Afia seemed to be a match made in Heaven. A divorce why?"

Kofi was embarrassed to say. "Apparently my dad's been cheating on my mom. They had this big ass argument about it the other night. Matter of fact, it was right after the game. Then me and my dad had a discussion about it later on that night. I don't know what to think. It honestly got me thinking about wanting to be single forever and just living my life on my own," Kofi explained. "And on top of that, it makes me want to leave home. I'm ready to move out. The end of year can't come fast enough."

"That's what all this was about? You could've just told me that without all the extra theatrics. I'm your friend. We're supposed to care about each other's struggles and mental health especially," Jerrod stressed.

Kofi appreciated that and admitted that he was out of line. "I fucked up on that. I took shit too far. My bad, bro." The two sat up as they continued their conversation.

"There could be a bright side to the situation but that depends on how you look at it."

Kofi wanted Jerrod to expound.

"How?"

"Because. It could be worse. There's kids out whose parents divorced at a younger age. Even before reaching their teenage years. At least you're fortunate to understand for that reason alone. It's not much of a big deal. I mean, we all want our parents to stay together forever in the same household, but it don't always play out like that."

Jerrod had a point. Kofi was intelligent enough to understand his parent's relationship.

"It may not have been that deep, but parents do need to be mindful, because a lot of shit can cause trauma, especially arguing in front of their kids. That's never been the wave. Don't get me wrong. I know it can get redundant and annoying when parents say it's not your fault. It's politically correct as hell, but the best way to look at it if they do get a divorced is the love will always be there for you, but ultimately, the happiness they want for themselves won't happen if they stay together," Jerrod continued.

Kofi witnessed unhappiness being torn apart by his dad's infidelity, and he didn't want to see his mom in a bad space emotionally and mentally. "This shit is just so hard. Just seeing her face of confusion and trying to find the answers on why my dad was moving the way he was."

Jerrod put his arm around Kofi. "Keep in mind that we're still young as hell. I'm sure your dad told you there's a dynamic you haven't reached or saw yet because you're not there yet to truly understand. Shit, I'm in the same boat from that perspective. We're young adults, and this is the time we're just discovering who we are with our feelings, and we're also sexually active. There's a way we have to handle them."

Kofi was holding back tears because his pride didn't want to show it. He felt that Afia was a genuine stone, and it was clear that Lance lost sight of that along the way or wanted a change. But Afia wasn't going to cause a wedge between a father and son.

"Everything will work itself out. What you need to do is just continue to focus on the remaining school year and your future post-graduation. This is miniscule, but you can't afford to let this be a burden on your heart," explained Jerrod.

"Say less," replied Kofi. "Now let's finish this

game and get the hell out of here. I was kicking your ass before you started acting crazy."

Kofi laughed it off and finished the game.

"Check the ball up," Jerrod ordered. "But hold up, whatever happened to the new girl at school that you was raving about?"

"Oh, you're talking about Liviana."

"Yeah."

"We're supposed to be chillin' soon. Since she's new to the state, I figure I show her around. I told her to have lunch with me," replied Kofi with a happy go luck smile. "Damn, why you making that face?"

"Just the conversations we've had a few times so far... she's funny and sarcastic. You know the feeling where a person makes you comfortable, and it's like you've known them forever? I wouldn't mind getting to know her more."

"Might be a good idea for you," suggested Jerrod.

"You think so for real?"

"Hell yeah. As much as you been knockin' off these chicks left and right, I bet you're exhausted with breaking hearts. She might be the one to tame your wild ass."

Kofi felt it wasn't a matter of being tamed but truly vibing with someone he felt a connection with.

"On a serious note. I did the same thing to her, but I wasn't as aggressive."

Jerrod was confused. "What you mean?"

"I saw her in a study hall, and we got to talking, and she said something, which in retrospect was just dry humor, and I got defensive. I couldn't bring myself to tell her about what was on my mind about my parents. She asked me if I was cool, and we don't even know each other. She had a genuine concern. That'll make anybody vulnerable in a good way," Kofi explained.

"You didn't tell one lie yet, especially because at the age we're at, we're in that infatuated phase and real feelings tend to get involved. That shit is scary," Jerrod added. "I'm cool, though. I rather keep myself sane by staying single."

The friends dapped each other up and left the gym.

Meanwhile, Afia was on the balcony enjoying the weather with a drink in her hand. She was quiet, and she was listening to the birds chirping. She always was a nature woman since she was a child. She picked up her phone and scrolled to research about divorce lawyers. Her mind was made up that she wanted to go her separate ways with Lance. She was still holding it together emotionally. The thought of staying crept in the back of her mind for the sake of Kofi, but she snapped out of those feelings because she didn't want to be weak. What pissed Afia off when she thought more about her devastation of being betrayed and trampled on was the fact that Lance continued to leech off Afia for his own selfish satisfaction instead of leaving the relationship if he was unhappy. She refused to drown in misery or be brainwashed into thinking he was going to change. She was a firm believer in karma and that it would come back full circle for the wrongdoings.

No sooner than she was getting the information she needed to pursue the divorce, Afia heard the door open, and it was Lance. She turned around, saw him, and gave an ice cold look while continuing to scroll through her phone. He walked in slowly bracing himself. She could hear his footsteps getting closer to coming to the backdoor to the balcony. She put her sunglasses on. Lance didn't know what to say, and Afia could feel him standing right beside her.

"What do you want?" she asked. "You're just looking at me."

Lance cleared his throat. "I think we should do couple's therapy."

Afia, at first, didn't react. She paused for a moment, and she gave out a dry laugh. "You're joking, right?"

"No. Not at all. I'm serious. We need to go to couple's therapy," repeated Lance.

Afia laughed once more, but her smile didn't reach her eyes. She was masking herself, but she took her sunglasses off and folded her arms. "And why is that?"

"Because I believe we can work though the bull-shit," replied Lance.

"You mean to tell me you can fuck another man's wife for god knows how long, look up escorts, and possibly pay them to fuck, and come home to me like everything is fine? Are you insane?"

Lance put his hands on his hip in frustration. "This is bullshit. See, this is the reason I can't talk to you about shit."

Afia turned to Lance's direction in an annoyed fashion. "You're not going to come in here and dictate what's bullshit. Because you wanna know what? You're assuming you have command to be in power in this situation. You don't. My courage has been saved up enough to walk away from you. That means I want a divorce. Let's just not waste our time. I don't have time to grieve right now. I love you, but I have to love myself. You have infatuations that evidently are more important than your wife and the mother of your son... Your only son."

"You must have another man on your mind." Lance was desperate for a reaction, and Afia didn't pay it no mind.

"You know what? You'll soon realize that your betrayal is my blessing," she said proudly. "You can't dominate me or manipulate me. You were out here doing whatever it was you pleased while I sat in this house being a good ass wife by being understanding of your career and being supportive. Quite frankly, after the tears I cried when I would ask myself what the fuck I was doing wrong, the only thing I could come up with was you'll be making my life better by walking out of it."

Lance wasn't going for it. "You're being narcissistic right now."

Afia covered her mouth again before silently laughing, and her shoulders shook in the process.

"Listen, I'm smart enough to know when you're projecting your bitterness and fuck ups on me, my love. I'm tired."

Lance folded his arms. "And you believe divorce is the best option? Don't you think you're being unreasonable and irrational about this shit?"

"Do you have any other splendid ideas? You're sitting here trying to flip it on me by trying to blame me for your behaviors, Lance. I can't do anything but take what you say with a grain of salt, and I thought you were better than that." Afia got up from her chair and moved to the other side of the balcony. "It sucks, doesn't it?"

"What does?"

"You know... not having that control. I do want what's best for you, too. I can hate you, but that's the route I'm going to take. Make yourself feel better for how you betrayed me and this family. One thing for sure is we will raise our son to be a fine young man that he already is, and I'll let go of the rest of you."

What made Afia livid about Lance was they were too old for the nonsense and that Lance should've known better that the grass wasn't always greener on the other side to jeopardize what he had at home. She walked away from Lance.

When Afia walked away, Lance's phone vibrated. Diana texted him. He saw Afia grab her keys and walk out of the door.

"Afia... wait."

She slammed the door on her way out.

While she was in the car, she called a divorce attorney. She knew it would possibly be an uphill battle, and she was nervous about it. The attorney at law she called told her he would draw a plan up to get straight to business when she got office to discuss what exactly she wanted from the divorce. He was firm and wanted to make sure her decision to file was the best choice because of the cost. She wanted to know about the legal options she had and go from there.

Chapter Six
Inexplicable Tears

I t was the month of the December. The second week of the month went by, and the tension was still thick in the Dixon household. With the parent's not getting along. Lance finally decided to move out, which became hard on Kofi, but Lance surprisingly wasn't petty enough to try to kick Afia out. He gave Afia space and didn't want to bother her. Kofi would often go over there and spend the night with Lance when he wanted to. He was back and forth between both residences. Afia always maintained the home.

While Lance was at his home, he heard a knock at the door.

"Who is it?" he asked, but nobody said anything. He got closer, and then the doorbell rang. "I asked who is it!" He looked out the window before opening the door, and he noticed that it was a County sheriff. "Can I help you with something, sir?"

"Yes, sir, you can. Lance Dixon?"

"I am."

The sheriff handed Lance an envelope, and he opened it up fast.

"You have been served. Have a good rest of the day," said the sheriff as he walked away.

Lance's face turned white. He was pissed but shut the door slowly trying to grasp that it was finally it... the divorce was a real thing. He threw the paper in the air and walked off. Lance grabbed a beer out of his refrigerator. To him, there was no point of fighting for the marriage when he was a serial cheater. Lance dialed Afia's number, and it rang a couple of times before she answered.

"Yeah?" she asked.

"I just had an interesting encounter at my door. The sheriff was just here an dropped off the divorce papers."

"Excellent. I'll be getting with my attorney so he can get in touch with yours, and we can get this ball rolling. I mean, that is whenever you hire an attorney. Also, I don't want Kofi involved with anything. This is between us. No support devices and attorneys will be speaking to him at all," lectured Afia. "Basically, what I'm saying, just so we're clear, is I want him to stay with me. I don't want this to be ugly and getting a judge involved and him having to testify about shit."

Lance understood. "Why didn't you just give these to me yourself?"

Afia scoffed before answering. "That wasn't an option. Plus, I didn't have the burning desire to see your facial expression once I gave it to you. Like I told you before, I'm not allowing you to control this situation. I want it over and done with."

Lance felt stripped of his pride, but he caused the mess. She suggested that Lance complied before it got worse legally, and that the attorney would be in a position to file motion for default judgement. It was in Lance's best interest to participate before he bit off more than he could possibly chew.

"You're enjoying this shit. What if I don't respond?" Lance kept trying to poke the bear.

"I'm not enjoying anything. Don't make this hard. You think I'm not hurting? Because I am. We can just do the paperwork ourselves, but I refuse to fight with you."

Lance agreed. He respected and greeted Afia's wishes. The best bet was to divide the assets and be adults instead of fight for superficial love that barely existed anymore. In her heart, Afia knew Lance was set in his ways, and he didn't want to be married, but he was rather comfortable. He wasn't who she fell in love with anymore.

The plan was to have everything in order by the end of the month and to possibly have the divorce completed in six weeks. Lance had sixty days tops to respond.

"For what it's worth, I didn't think I'd ever be in this position because I was taught that divorce was frowned upon in my culture and that you remain by your husband's side no matter what. You as a man are supposed to respect what I want and let it be up to me if I want to leave or stay. I want out." Afia didn't have much more to say about it until the divorce was finalized in court. "I gotta go. Just play your part. My attorney will be in touch."

She hung up abruptly before Lance could reply to her. He tossed the phone on his couch.

Kofi was having lunch with Afia at Seaspice. It was long overdue to have a mother and son time. It was a nice day outside. Kofi was in the mood for some Jumbo Shrimp cocktail. The service was fast. As soon as the waiter brought his food, he didn't waste any time digging in. "

Is your food good?" asked Afia jokingly.

"I was starving." Kofi laughed.

Afia took a drink of her water and enjoyed the atmosphere. "Graduation is soon here. Are you ready?"

"I been ready. Right around the corner, but the sad part about high school is that some students that I been around for all four years I'll never see them again, unfortunately. Everybody going their separate ways. That's the only depressing part. There's a lot I'm going to miss, so I'm cherishing these last couple months," he explained.

"Make sure you buy a yearbook and have as many people sign it as possible to reflect on those points in your life."

Kofi agreed. He was nervous about shifting the conversation to the divorce controversy.

"True, but listen, Mom. I know this might be bad timing, and it's not what you wanna hear right now, and it's also random, but all things considered, I do respect and admire the courage you showed to walk away. This hurts, and I know it's complicated, and maybe I really don't understand fully, but I know the feeling of moving forward no matter what the odds are in front of you," explained Kofi.

"Thank you, son."

"Are you gonna be okay?"

"Yes. I will be. One of the lessons, and not just in marriages or divorces, but in life, is that you only have one life. As long as I keep telling myself that, I'll be on the right track. I'm in control of my destiny. As days and months go by, I'll get used to being by myself again, and I don't mean that in a bad way." Kofi grabbed a hold of his mother's hand. Afia quickly grabbed the paper towel on the table to wipe her eyes. She wasn't ashamed to cry in front of her son. "I shared majority of my life with your father, but I'm not sinking and drowning in misery. My mind just needs to rest in the meantime."

While Afia smiled, trying to keep her emotional armor on, her eyes told a different story when she spoke. Her eyes remained tearful and damp. There wasn't much Kofi could do besides letting her emotions run their course. She was aware that Kofi was sexually active and that he wasn't with just one girl. He had his curiosity with Liviana, but they weren't taking each other personally at the time.

"Will this happen to me?"

"Will what happen to you?"

"I can't predict the future, but If I get married, will I do the same things as Dad? I cared for a lot of girls in my life so far, but what if I'm in a position where I feel something is missing, but I'm with the one I love? What if I'm wired to just like new things? Does that make me a bad guy?"

"No, sweetheart, it doesn't make you bad guy at all. We're all flawed and also have to give ourselves grace," she replied.

Kofi thpught about the idea of love and if his life would be set up as a novel experience and not truly being committed once he tied the knot by mirroring his father. He had a long bridge to cross, but his mind always wandered. He took a sip of his drink, sat his plate to the side, and spaced out momentarily.

Afia gently grabbed Kofi's chin. "Baby boy, just know your personality determines the path you take physically and emotionally. And don't you ever forget that. Relationships are complicated. Things can go downhill fast once someone loses their faith in you."

Kofi always asked questions. "I know it's uncomfortable to talk about it because it's fresh situation, and since I'm young, I know I'm not the best resource to vent to, Mom. I feel like I'll have to brace myself for unexpected anger from you," he explained.

"I'll have my moments, but I'll get there. Trust my process. The world isn't going to end. I've stumbled through a painful situation."

Kofi wanted to be the one to motivate both his parents. He wanted to be the sun after the storm.

"I got your back, Mom."

Afia's eyes shimmered. "Thank you, son. I needed to hear those words."

Indirectly and not realizing she was doing so, Afia leaned on Kofi for backup. Her support system wasn't the greatest, but she was making it work. She was broken for the time being, but she was ready to be reborn.

It was the new year, and the divorce was close to being done. Lance and Afia remained amicable, but it was still emotionally exhausting. Luckily, both Afia and Lance had their attorneys that moved the process at a good pace to get it over with. They constantly kept in touch if anything changed. They agreed that mediation was the best bet. Since divorce was expensive and took patience, Afia drilled her head with as much information on the family law just in case Lance might start to be unreasonable for alimony purposes. The smartest thing she did during the time was put together her own divorce papers. She was great at drafting. She kept her king heart and didn't prolong her healing process. She even went on a few dates to pass the time but nothing at all was exclusive. She remained content with initiating the divorce and that helped her go through the emotions and prevented her from being a train wreck. She was up for the task of starting a new life on her own and continuing her career. Her career kept her busy and on her feet. They didn't want a trial for the divorce to have a resolution. It stayed at being secluded, and Kofi wasn't going to be there to watch or be in the middle.

Afia's attorney looked over her draft and made sure it was solid before anything was signed off. She wanted to keep her name. All necessary paperwork was signed. A weight was just lifted off Afia's shoulder.

"It's all done," her attorney said.

She put her head down, and she got teary eyed.

"What about your son?" asked the Lance's attorney.

"He's of age to choose who he wants to live with technically, but he's going to stay with his mother unless she gives the blessing that he can live with his father if she allows it. No line in the sand will be drawn between Mr. Dixon and his son," explained Afia's attorney.

Lance, Afia, and both lawyers stood up at once.

"Best wishes," said Afia's lawyer, and Lance shook his lawyer's hand.

After walking out of the room, Lance stopped Afia in her tracks. "Glad that went well, right?" asked Lance, making conversation.

"I guess so, yes."

There was an awkward silence.

"Obviously whenever Kofi wants to come over, he can."

"Indeed. You're his father. Absolutely."

"Not surprised that it came to this conclusion," Lance added.

"Right. It became more bad times than good. It

was draining to have to keep going with this. I won't lie and say there were little voices in my head telling me to ride this out with you, but knowing it was withering and both of us would've been lying to ourselves that we were happy and in love. Maybe emotionally and physically you were depleted, but we could've talked about how the romance cooled down. There's a lot of things I don't feel like rehashing anymore. We have to keep a relationship somewhat because of Kofi, so we don't have to worry about going at each other's throats for the sake of being argumentative."

"I get it. You're right, but I don't regret my history with you. You gave me a precious gift, and I'm forever grateful for that eternally."

Afia respected that Lance didn't use their son as a weapon of revenge to gain control or make accusations that were false to ramp up emotions out of Afia. She commended him for that. "Thanks, but this was good, because now I don't feel endangered," she added.

"What does that mean?"

"Because, Lance, I wasn't going to go another damn day in a marriage that isn't right for my mental health. It just wasn't conducive anymore. If it isn't right for me, then I need to walk away. The decisions you made, you stood on those decisions. You need to change your ways before it comes back to bite you in your ass. You have a good day," said Afia with relief and a big smile on her face when she left the building., leaving Lance standing there watching her walk away.

Kofi had a free day where he had nothing going on after school. It was rare that he didn't have anything on the schedule. He was lying on his bed scrolling through his phone on social media. He had many inboxes from different females that wanted to link up with him, but he wasn't in the mood for it. He decided to give it a shot to text Liviana to see what she was up to. They texted for a few minutes, and then Kofi called her.

"Hey... What's up?"

"Well, hello. This was unexpected."

"Damn. There goes my self-este"m," he replied. "Maybe I just wanted to hear your voice. What are you up to? Are you busy?"

"Nothing much. How about yourself?"

"I had some free time today, so I figure we could possibly hang out."

"I like the sound of that. What did you have in mind?"

"It's a nice day out. Let's go grab some food. I also planned on getting a pair of new sneakers, so we could go to mall if you'd like to tag along? But first, I wanna show you a dope place to eat, and it's my favorite spot."

Liviana let Kofi know it sounded like a plan.

"Send me your address if you're cool with that, and I'll pick you up."

Liviana texted Kofi the address. He didn't live but twenty minutes away.

"I'll be there soon."

Kofi waited for Liviana to come outside as he listened to music. It was seventy-five degrees out. Livana came outside, and Kofi watched her walking off the porch to his car. She had on light blue jeans, a pair of white Adidas, and a white vintage long sleeve shirt. She embraced the plain look for that day. Her hair was curly, and she had a gold chain on. Kofi smelled her scent right away. When she got inside the car, he turned the music volume down.

"Oh wow. What's that fragrance that you got on?" he asked right away.

"Victoria's Secret Bare," she replied.

Not only was the scent unique but clean and fresh.

"Wow, that smells amazing."

"Thank you."

"Do you have an appetite? Because I'm hungry as hell."

"Yes. Where to?"

"It's for me to know and you find out." Kofi gave out a playful wink in a flirtatious manner.

Liviana was amused by Kofi as she looked away and folded her arms with a slight grin on her face. While they were driving, Kofi cracked the windows to feel a small breeze. While his music was playing, he made mini dance gestures. Liviana loved his vibe.

They pulled up to the spot where Kofi was taking Liviana. Kofi told Liviana to wait so he could open her door for her. The restaurant they came to was The Big Easy Winebar and Grill.

"You'll love this food, trust me," said Kofi enthusiastically. He rubbed his hands together in excitement. "They have the best food ever!"

The two sat down.

"Tell me what's good here."

"I'm glad you said that. The black & bleu burger is good, and so are the bayou fries with crab and cheese. You won't be disappointed."

Liviana took his word for it. "Okay. The crispy sandwich burger sounds good, too."

The waitress took their orders, and it didn't take long for them to get their food. Kofi raved about his crawfish fries, stuffing his face. While the average girl would've been turned off by the gluttonous gesture, Liviana knew he was being funny.

"Damn. Slow down before you choke."

"I can't help it. I love this spot." Kofi gave Liviana a teasing smile.

She was trying to keep her cool, but every time Kofi looked in her eyes, she felt useless and giggled bashfully.

"There we go!" said Kofi.

He made Liviana feel a connection. She felt enticed.

"How's life been the last two months since you've been in Miami? I bet you're missing Atlanta."

"It's been well. Still homesick, but I'm managing," she replied.

"I've been keeping my mind distracted lately. Being here with you helps. I didn't feel like being home. I needed time to unwind. No school stuff, you feel me? Just a peace of mind."

"Hmm. Why do you feel that way?"

Kofi breathed through his nose and gathered himself. "My parents are getting a divorce, so it's been tough not having them both in the house. I noticed that my mom was miserable," he explained.

"Why are they getting a divorce?" Liviana could feel the disappointment from Kofi.

"My dad was cheating on my mom, and she found out. It all went downhill from there."

Liviana felt bad. "I can't imagine the stress level you might be under with that. I'm sorry."

Kofi shrugged his shoulders and exhaled. "It's about being happy, so it's not about me. It's about them. My dad fumbled. But my dad is still my homie. I'm torn."

"You know giving the support is the best in those types of situations. Maybe even writing about it in a journal by addressing your emotions. It should help you for a life changing event ou have no control of."

"That's actually not a bad idea. I agree on that. I know I'm not a lil' kid, but now it'll be weird when it's time to celebrate my birthday, and they'll be separated. It feels like I have to create a whole new life." Anytime Kofi was feeling an emotion, he had to let out a release.

"I'm sure they'll put their pride to the side for you," Liviana added. "Gotta give it time to adjust, which I'm sure they told you. It sucks when your parents ain't a unit anymore."

Kofi was curious about Liviana's home life. "What about you? Are you parent's still together?"

"No, they're not."

"Do you have any siblings, or are you an only child?"

"It's just me, but it's not a bad thing. I used to think I would get lonely, but it blew over with time." Liviana had a love and hate relationship with her father. He didn't want to move to Miami, so he stayed in Atlanta. She went through a rollercoaster due to her father being a drug addict who picked and chose when he wanted to be in her life. The best decision was to keep her distance for the time being, even though she spoke to him from time to time, but it wasn't fair for her to have to deal with inconsistency.

"At least I'm not the only one whose an only child," said Kofi after finishing up the rest of his food as did Liviana. "Was I right? Was the food what I said it was gonna be?"

Kofi pulled his money out to pay, and he also tipped the waitress.

"You have good taste. You weren't lying and thank you for bringing me here. I'll have to come here with you again."

"I'm down. Just say the word, and we can set it up," Kofi said with confidence. "Now that we're full, what do you say if we do a little bit of shopping? I'm not ready to let you go just yet."

Liviana was loving her time with Kofi. "You're the driver. Looks like I'm stuck with you. Let's go. What's the mall out here called?"

"There's too many, but I wanted to check out Miami Design District."

Liviana was intrigued. "What do they have down there?" she asked curiously.

"All types of stores. You'll see luxurious cars driving by. It's a great place to explore. Not sure if you're into art, but they have art galleries, and it's filled with clothing shopping centers. All the latest. Smooth place for entertainment. It's a beautiful day, so we might as well make the best of it, right?"

"Yes. Let's go."

Lance's phone rang, and it was Diana calling. He let it ring and contemplated on not answering, but he gave in. "Hello?"

"Hi, baby. Why haven't I heard from you?"

"Is that a trick question? I just been laying low. Don't you think that's the best option since we've already been caught by both our spouses for fuckin' around?" Diana gave out a sharp bark of laughter, and Lance didn't find anything funny at all. "You think this is the time to be joking? It's bad enough that me and your husband work together, and we've already had a run in. We can't make shit worse. I'm fresh off my divorce, and you're still a married woman."

"Married, yes, but not happily," she answered. Lance was wondering why Diana didn't just get a divorce her damn self. "Why are you acting scared, Lance? What is it? What? You don't miss lickin' these juices? No point of having a guilty conscious now. We're both homewreckers. We're just taking a ride on the wild side, boo boo."

Lance scratched his head and thought long and hard on his urges. Diana told Lance that Malcolm was out playing poker with his friends and wouldn't be back until later at night.

"Look, just come over. She needs you bad. He won't even know you were here, so just bring your ass over, and give me that fat veiny dick. I wanna suck out every last bit of semen you can produce."

Once again, Lance gave in. "Fuck it! I'm on my way."

Lance was over in thirty minutes. When he arrived, he sat in his car for a few minutes before exiting. Even though he was violating again with risking going inside a married man's home, he was horny as fuck and took his chances.

Lance knocked on the door softly. He didn't want to be too loud. She answered the door after she got finished pouring herself a drink of wine. The moment she saw Lance, she got wet through her panties. She jumped in his arms right away. He had a grip on her ass cheeks as they kissed. He grabbed her arms and pushed her back. "Let me ask you something."

"Shut the fuck up, and kiss me. Don't kill the moment."

"I'm serious. I need to know what we're doing in the long term."

"You can ask me anything," Diana said as she nibbled on Lance's neck and brushed her lips over his ear. She was looking at his physique. She touched his face and was about to lean in for another kiss until he stepped back.

"Hold on. Maybe I should go. Your husband could show up at any time. I don't have time to deal with that shit."

Diana wasn't taking Lance seriously. It was a dangerous gamble going on for a night of sexual gratification, and Diana was willing to take her chances.

"Please. You're already here. Your ass isn't going anywhere. Not on my watch." Diana was convincing. She turned around and got behind him and placed her hands inside his pants. "Come on. You don't wanna leave, do you, baby?" asked Diana with a sinister face. In a sick way, Diana flirted with the idea of getting caught by her husband. Lance erected fast. "It's fun to break the rules. Come be my partner in crime," she whispered in his ear. "You wanna be a superhero for the night, or are you gonna continue to be stupid?"

That made Lance turn around and face her. "Stupid?"

Diana was trying to get Lance riled up and pissed off so he could fuck her insides up. Lance snatched Diana up and aggressively kissed her. From how he reacted when she insulted him, more of a flood arrived in her panties. She gasped as she was put off balance.

"It's about fuckin' time! Yes! That's what I'm talkin' about!"

He ran his hands through her hair and proceeded to run his arms across her thighs after he pulled her closer to him. Lance was ready to get busy as his dick was trying to escape his pants. It was growing through his pants, making him uncomfortable. His blood was flowing. Lance shoved his tongue down Diana's throat while they rubbed and swirled their tongues together in a graceful motion. They heaved and moaned. All hell was about to break loose. Diana pushed her bedroom door open. Lance ripped everything off.

. . .

An hour passed, and Lance and Diana were fucking up the bed sheets like there was no tomorrow. What they didn't realize was Malcolm was on his way home from playing poker. He was tired. It was one in the morning. It was a sober night for him because he didn't want to get pulled over. Malcolm was walking up to his house and heard noises that sounded like screaming. He noticed the light in his bedroom was on, and from where he was standing, he could see shadows moving back and forth from the lighting. At first, he was thinking Diana might've been in trouble. Malcolm gently opened the screen door and unlocked the door slowly to creep in. While he was at the front of the steps, he could hear the bed creaking.

Diana had a big ass mouth, but she couldn't help it because her personality was extroverted. She was loud. While Lance was inside of her and thrusting, Diana was vociferous. She went from screaming to holding her breathe to her face being contorted, which made her cum and convulse to the point she forced Lance out of her. Lance relaxed and it pushed himself deeper inside Diana. She yelped uncontrollably as he slid his tongue across her cheek. Diana's walls strengthened up as Lance's dick punched her cervix. She squeezed tightly, and her titties swelled at the crest of her next orgasm.

"Ahh! Motherfucker! Yes!" she hollered as her eyes rolled to the back of her head.

The sounds Diana made validated the work Lance was putting in. His skills spoke high volumes. Lance and Diana had no idea that Malcolm crept inside the house and walked to the steps silently. They didn't hear a peep. Malcolm couldn't bring himself to see what was going on yet. All he could do was silently sob while hearing his wife panting and groaning.

By this time, Diana was on her third peak. She let out one more final squeal before Malcolm kicked the door off the hinges and the latch. The door had a soft wood frame, so it was easy to break the doorframe around the latch to catch Lance and Diana off guard.

Lance and Diana jumped out of the bed. Lance used the pillow to cover himself and stood in the corner. He was expecting Malcolm to make a move on him to start fighting him, but Malcolm didn't budge yet. He looked at the bed and saw the creamy white fluid that was soaked on the black bed sheets. Malcolm was emotionally horrified when he saw how thick and creamy her sex juices were on the bed that he paid for. He couldn't fathom why Diana would scontinue to blatantly disregard his feelings after the countless times he told her to stop having an affair. Diana thought her husband was a simp with no backbone. Angry was an understatement, but he was composed after wiping his tears. Malcolm stared back and forth at the two.

Malcolm didn't feel like raising his voice. Little did Lance and Diana know, he was already formulating a plan in his head to get rid of both of them forever. A plan he told himself he wouldn't do if he was in a position of catching his wife. Malcolm could be a ticking time bomb but didn't grant Lance the satisfaction of knowing that yet. Diana thrived off drama.

"You fucked up," said Malcolm as he pointed at Diana. Her being humble enough to acknowledge he faults was nonexistent. "This is how you do me? Right in my own fuckin' house?"

Malcolm had his fists balled up.

"Don't you yell at me!" screamed Diana.

Ironically, Malcolm remained poised. She was reaching for a reaction. The card was already shown while Malcolm was still hiding his feelings.

"Seems like neither one of you have learned anything... I bust my motherfuckin' ass every day to provide for you and the rest of this family. I work late, I sacrifice, and all I wanted was to be treated with respect. Was that too much to ask for, you dumb bitch?"

Diana had her arms folded while Malcolm was spitting venom from his voice. Diana waived Malcolm off. She and Lance looked at each other. Lance directed his eyes on Malcolm. Subconsciously, he was preparing for a physical altercation with him. It was nothing like the calm before the storm.

Lance let out a laugh, but it rang hollow.

"Are you done with your little speech now?" asked Diana.

As dangerous as it was to remain at the house, Malcolm stayed instead of packing his bags and booking a hotel for a while until things cooled off and he figured out a healthy plan on where his next domicile was going to be. The final straw was already reached, unfortunately.

"Don't stop now. Keep going. Pretend I'm not even here." Malcolm's rage was decisive.

"You know what? I'm not dealing with this, Malcolm."

Malcolm gestured toward Lance. "You think you're getting a free pass?"

Lance got his clothes on to leave out smoothly.

He didn't want to be lured into a fight, even though Malcolm was visibly being antagonized by Diana.

"Where you think you're going, motherfucker? We're not done here yet. The fuck did you think this was?"

Lance stopped. "You're not done, but I'm done."

"I just wanted to thank you. I'm feeling real generous tonight. I think I should buy you gift."

Lance was confused. "What the fuck are you talking about?"

"Thank you for taking this trifling bitch off my hands. She's your problem now. I can't handle any more deceit from her stupid ass."

Diana was proof that accountability could be a woman's kryptonite.

"What are you even doing? You're just making a fool of yourself." She was trying her hardest to strip away Malcolm's masculine frame. She underestimated how terrible events could take a turn for the worst when being betrayed. Diana was putting her bra back on and her panties.

"Wait. Where do you think you're going?" Diana asked Lance, who was creeping out of the room.

"What the fuck kind of question is that? I'm getting the fuck out of here. I knew this was a bad idea. You and him can deal with this shit on your own time, but I'm out."

Malcolm's soul was destroyed. He went down to the kitchen, and he retrieved a butcher's knife. He looked at it before leaving the kitchen to head back to bedroom. He could hear Lance and Diana still talking. They were blissfully unaware of the current state of emotional destruction that Malcolm felt. He walked back up on a mission. Lance heard the footsteps again.

"Look, I gotta go before he does something stupid."

But before he could leave the room, Malcolm was already in the hallway and pointed the knife at Lance's face.

"Get the fuck back in the room!" Malcolm screamed at the top of his lungs.

"Whoa! Whoa! Take it easy!" Lance screamed back.

Just like Lance, Malcolm was in tip top shape.

"Fuck that!" Diana backed herself in the corner of her side of the bed. Her cocky attitude changed from dismissive and arrogant to scared, and Malcolm noticed her mood switch.

"What's the matter, baby? Your whore ass had so much shit to say earlier." He played with knife like a cat about to play with a mouse before eating it. He was thinking about who he wanted to attack first.

The sad thing was, Malcolm always portrayed himself as a wholesome gentleman who was hard working and faithful, but now, he was derailed and unstable.

"You're taking shit too far. I think you need to relax," suggested Lance. "It doesn't have to be like this."

It was the audacity to Malcolm, but Lance kept his hands up.

"What doesn't it have to be like, exactly? Huh? Are you fuckin' with my head right now?" Malcolm didn't feel like letting karma handle the situation on its own. He was a lost cause. He wanted to handle it differently for his sadistic enjoyment of physical pain instead. "One moment," he said, while locking the door.

Lance was about to fight it out. As soon as the door locked, Lance lunged at Malcolm, and they started to scuffle. The knife was the near the end of the bed where it fell when he hit Malcolm. A series of punches were thrown, and the men were wrestling for the knife when it eventually fell off the bed.

Unfortunately, Malcolm got the best of Lance. He punched him in the face again. He was in daze while Malcolm retrieved the knife and was about to stab him. Lance was able to grab his arm to stop from being stabbed right away. Malcolm was getting closer to his chest. Sure enough, Malcolm gave him a demonic dagger to his chest, right to the heart. Lance yelled from the impact of the knife being plunged inside him. Blood left his body, and he started hemorrhaging before he passed out, giving Malcolm unimpeded access to his body. Diana screamed while Malcolm butchered Lance. He cut through his blood vessels. He sawed him in and out. Blood squirted in the air.

Diana couldn't move as she saw Lance being hacked right in front of her eyes. She didn't feel she had a clear path to run. Her legs wouldn't move, and she was too frightened to make a run for the door. It didn't help that the door was locked, and she'd be taking time off by trying to unlock it. Diana's fun quickly turned into a massacre right before her eyes. Lance's leg jiggled. Malcolm slowly stood up and placed the knife on the dresser gently. Diana had a sharp change in heartbeat when Malcolm rose up. Her throat was constricted.

"You're next." Malcolm ran at a fast pace to grab

Diana by the throat, banging her head against the mirror, which broke. Malcolm then slammed her on her back, picking her back up, and pushed her against the wall. Diana's vision was blurry, and she instantaneously became weak and coughed. Malcolm wanted to torment her. He slung her around the room and jumped on top of her. He strangled her. She struggled to get words out.

"Malc..." She coughed again.

"What did you say?" He let go, but she was still pinned to the floor. "I can't understand you, my love. Speak up! Are you having trouble breathing?"

"Yes! Daddy, do it harder!" she hollered back. Diana was under pressure to stay alive. She was trying to hit Malcolm with a Jedi mind trick to get to freedom by throwing him off.

She was using arousal tactic. She moaned, which was uncanny, but her attempt on survival wasn't supposed to be glorious. Her life just depended on it. The sexual fashions weren't working. Diana was fighting her ass off. She kneed Malcolm in his groin to make a run for it. He grunted while grabbing himself in agony.

"Ugh! Bitch!" He was hurt.

She threw up mucus and tonsil stones were on the floor. The scuffle happened so fast. For a few seconds, blood was able to rush back to Diana's brain. She tried to make a run for the door but slipped on Lance's blood while screaming at the same time. She was too distraught to conserve her breath. Malcolm was able to grab her leg and drag her to middle of the bedroom floor. He smacked her in the face and placed his hands back on her neck to finish her off.

"You shouldn't have done that! You made me do this, Diana!" Malcolm hollered with a menacing undertone. He was using all his might. Diana's face was petrified. He was reveling in her terror, getting pleasure in how scared and helpless she was at that moment.

Malcolm was strangling Diana's life away. She gasped for air. She tried to gouge Malcolm's nose and eyes with her fingernails but barely could reach them. He continued to torment, and he calmly shed a tear that dropped from his cheek onto her face. Her tongue was out. She was trying her best to alleviate pressure to buy more time to live. She clawed at his hands next, which infuriated him more.

"Why the fuck won't you die?"

She tried one more time to gouge Malcolm's eyes and was temporarily successful at stunning him. Her whole world spun, and he was too persistent.

She was fully aware that she was about to die but was gunning for some type of peace. She closed her eyes. Malcolm's grip on her neck was just too powerful. Her body couldn't take it anymore. By this time, Diana's air supply was cut off from Malcolm pressing her blood vessels on the side of her throat, making her larynx break in the process. Diana's time was expired.

Malcolm looked at Diana's neck and saw the bruises and the marks he left on her face when he smacked her. Malcolm kissed her dead lips. "Bye, love."

After the murders were done, Malcolm was sad and distraught. He stood up and looked at the brutal scene inside the bedroom. He walked over to Lance's body, grabbed the knife, and pointed it in his face, noticing Lance's eyes were open. Malcolm wiped his face from the blood and the sweat.

"Look at you now, you bitch ass nigga! Under any circumstances, never underestimate someone's ability to kill you!" Malcolm hollered at both lifeless bodies. Malcolm laughed but was hurting inside and desperately cried through a sheer amount of pain and anger from Lance and Diana. He felt justified and provoked.

"You know how long I've been waiting for this?

And now the plate was right in front of me? Look at you both! You're dead!"

Lance's arrogance and disrespect killed him because he took Malcolm for a joke. Diana was a classic example of playing stupid games and paying with her life. There wasn't any point of cleaning up the mess that was made. Malcolm was lost. He was psychologically pleased with the chaos as he bragged, enjoying the fruits of his labor, but after ten minutes when he sat on the bed, reality finally set in. He was fucked. His life was over.

Malcolm walked down the steps and opened the front door. He had his cell phone in his bloody hand and sat on the porch. He was panting. The knife was still in his hand. He dialed 911 to confess about what he just did. He explained the details over the phone all while sobbing at the same time.

"I killed my wife! I killed my wife! Please get here as fast as you can. My wife is upstairs in the bedroom along with another man. They're both dead." Malcolm knew he was vile scum for what he did but was tired of turning the other check and confronted the situation in his own manner. He allowed Lance and Diana to steal his essence. Surrendering was the best solution, but in the back of his head, so was dying. Even with calling the cops on himself, he was wondering if he was going to be shot dead on sight or be took in custody without being harmed.

While he sat and waited for help, he contemplated his fate. Whether it was killing himself with the knife or suicide by cop. One thing for sure was he didn't want his worthless skin to be miserable in prison regardless.

The first responding officer pulled up, and ten minutes later, other patrol units raced to the scene. The first responding officer saw Malcolm brandishing the bloody knife. An ambulance was on the way, and the officer also called a homicide detective. The closer the cops came to the house, Malcolm became nervous. The cops could see how bloody his shirt was. He placed the knife on his neck. The first responding officer was trying to talk him down. Officers immediately drew their weapons in the event that Malcolm would rush one of the officers, and they would be forced to shoot his ass down off rip.

"Put it down, sir! Let's talk!" suggested the officer. "This isn't the way. I promise you it isn't. Don't make this worse!"

There were a few times Malcolm was hesitant and was poking himself, inflicting sharp pain on the side of his neck. His adrenaline was up, and he was testing the waters.

"Hey! Don't do that, sir!"

"It can't get any worse!" yelled Malcolm back to the officer. "I had to do it. They left me with no choice."

The officers were trying to keep him alive. He continued to try to justify his actions. He was growing more eager.

"No, sir! Don't do it! Just put the knife down."

"Tell my kids I'm sorry and that I love them!"

"No!" screeched the officers at the same time. Malcolm slit his throat with one quick motion and dropped to the ground. He sliced his carotid artery and severed his trachea. He was struggling and gargling blood.

The officers ran over and called for the medics. "We need medical assistance! Shit!"

Officers secured the scene, and that was where they found the bloodbath upstairs. They were horrified. Forensics, the detective, and the coroner were notified. They were on their way to the scene. While the environment was hectic and potentially contaminated, there weren't any witnesses found yet. It was an isolated incident done in the middle of the night. Photos were taken of the blood stains that sat on the bedroom floor. One of the officers felt like he was about to throw up. A detective by the name of Keith Copeland just pulled up. He walked up to the room and looked at the surroundings. The first guess was that it wasn't a premeditated murder by Malcolm. The cops told Copeland there might've been a heated exchange before the murders occurred. Lance's pockets had all his identification in it.

"Hmm. Lance Dixon. That name sounds familiar," said Copeland as he snapped his fingers, trying to recollect who Lance was. "The man told dispatch that he killed his wife. He was frantic over the phone, sir."

By this time, the bodies in the bedroom were being covered up.

"I can see that. That's evident," responded Copeland. "He most likely caught them both by surprise. The officers checked all through the house for anymore possible victims and evidence, but between the bedroom and front porch where Malcolm's body was, there wasn't anybody else."

"Alright, so this is what we're gonna do. We're gonna keep searching this damn house to make sure everything is compatible with what the hell we see right here. Somebody bring me a coffee. Shit, this man is carved. The gentleman was pissed the fuck off. And you can tell by this woman's neck that she was strangled hard. Does she have a name?"

"We're still trying to figure that out, sir. We haven't retrieved any identification yet."

"Okay. Keep canvassing. A few of you need to hit the kitchen. Search for cell phones and licenses. Look around for a purse from this woman, you understand me? Are the technicians on their way?"

"Yes, sir, they are," answered one of the officers.

"Perfect. Let's seal the house up until they get here. I need several officers to knock door to door for possible witness right now!" ordered Copeland. "Let's move!"

Copeland walked back out the front door, being careful.

Copeland ordered the team to get video and photos of the parked cars. After photographs were taken and the necessary procedures were in order, the bodies were then transported to the hospital.

Lance had fingerprints on a state database, so the police were able to figure out who to get in contact with to notify his family members. The medical examiner preferred that family wasn't told until twenty-four hours had passed by.

Once Copeland found out who it was, it finally

came to him, and he caught the fear of God. He got the awful feeling in his stomach because he realized that he knew Afia, and this was her husband, obviously unaware that they were divorced. Copeland and Afia worked together when she became a CSI and often saw her in passing. They built a rapport. The turn of events just got worse.

"Fuck..."

"What's wrong?" asked the medical examiner.

Copeland couldn't wait that long to tell Afia. It was part of the job to let her know.

"I know this man," said Copeland. "I mean... I know of him, but I know his wife. This is going be fun."

Afia was off. Often, she would be called in the middle of the night, but tonight, she wasn't. At the time, it was three in the morning, and Kofi and Afia were sleeping. Copeland walked up to the door and rang the doorbell. Afia yawned and slowly got out of bed. She put her slippers on, walked down the steps, and opened the door. She was surprised to see Copeland. "Keith, what are you doing here?"

"Hi, Afia. May I come in, please?" Copeland asked while trembling.

Afia was trying to wake up. "Yeah, come in. Is there something wrong?"

"I need you to sit down for this, please. It's about your husband."

"My husband? Me and Lance are divorced. What happened?"

Copeland was desperate to try to take way the initial pain of having to inform Afia of Lance's murder, but it was going to be shocking regardless. "Look, I apologize to have to inform you about this, but he passed away tonight."

Copeland felt like a piece of shit having to deliver that news to her in the middle of the night. He rather it been himself than a grieving counselor. Afia covered her mouth and stood up from the couch. She automatically thought about how Kofi was going to take it and that her son's future was stolen from him. Having both parents in life was equivalent to needing light and air. Afia saw grey in her vision and felt nauseous.

"Tell me what happened, Keith!" Afia already

knew that there was nothing she could do to fix the situation.

"He was at the Lawrence residence," replied Copeland.

"Who are the Lawrences?"

Copeland cleared his throat and choked on his spit. "We have reason to believe that he was over there with Diana Lawrence, who is the wife of Malcolm Lawrence. So far, from what we gathered, she was having an affair with Lance. He most likely caught them in a compromising position, and in return, he killed them."

Afia flopped back on the couch and stared at the ceiling. "This is unbelievable. This can't be true. There's no way this is possible." Afia couldn't close her eyes even if she wanted to at that moment. She told Copeland a month ago that she and Lance were divorced because of the cheating and that Malcolm confronted the situation to her, and she was even unsure how Malcolm was able to find her home.

"Our son is upstairs. How am I going to tell him that his father was killed tonight? Never in a million years did I think it would get this far!" Afia felt bad because she remembered when she talked to Lance about Karma coming back. "That man was angry, but he seemed like he was holding it together. He didn't give me vibes that he was going to kill him. If I would've saw any signs, I would've notified."

Kofi woke up because he had to go to the bathroom, and he was also thirsty. He heard voices downstairs, and he walked down the steps to see who it was.

"Mom, is that you? You good?" Kofi saw Detective Copeland. He didn't expect anybody to be down there at that time of night.

Afia was in total shock. She made her ways toward Kofi with tears in her eyes. Kofi's look was empty.

"Honey... Can you come sit with me, please?" she asked anxiously. Afia got a hold of Kofi's hand when he sat next to her.

"What is it, Mom? I have to wake up in like three hours."

Afia could see that she was scaring Kofi. She paused briefly and stuttered. "Your father was hurt tonight. It's bad."

Kofi's octave rose, and his eyes collapsed. "Wait... What do you mean? Bad how?"

Afia's eyes became more tearful, and she put her head down.

"Are you trying to tell me that Dad is... Dad is dead? Is this some type of fuckin' sick joke?"

"No, I'm afraid it isn't," answered Copeland. "I'm so sorry for your loss."

For a moment, Kofi spaced out while his eyes watered up. There was pain in his stomach that he never felt before. A knot was an understatement. More like a frozen sledgehammer. Kofi jumped up from the couch, but Afia quickly grabbed him and squeezed him as tightly as she could. Kofi hyperventilated, and his body was numb. Kofi couldn't do anything but soak his tears inside his mother's shirt while feeling a breathtaking emptiness.

Chapter Seven
Waves of Anxiety

Even though Lance was properly identified by his DNA records and tattoos he had on his body, Afia requested to see him one more time. Other family members were eventually notified about his death, and they were rushing to the hospital. Kofi was frantic and tried to run out the door.

They made their way to the hospital. Several nurses, the family, and security stayed with Kofi to watch over him. Nurses that were walking in the hallway could hear the commotion from Lance's death as family members were going off. They were acting a fool in the hospital. Helpless screams ripped through the hallways. Afia wasn't in the right mindset to explain what the exact reason was for Lance to be killed and the fact that he was murdered by not living by integrity. All Afia could feel was pure unadulterated rage.

Since it was ruled a homicide, she was guided to the room but couldn't touch him or go in. She had to look from the window. A nurse held Afia's hand and was comforting her when she was walking to where Lance was. She turned the corner and seen where he was placed with the white sheet over him. Afia didn't want Kofi to see his father like that, and it wouldn't bring much closure but rather make things worse. It wasn't a pleasurable feeling seeing faces of death because that would stick with him for years to come.

Afia shivered as she got closer to the window and the white sheet was slowly removed from Lance to reveal to Afia. She breathed at a fast rate and felt lightheaded.

"Oh my God... Nooo!" she screamed as she fell to the ground. "Lance, I'm so sorry!"

The nurse picked Afia up and hugged her tightly. The burst of tears wouldn't stop as a cloud rained over her. "Come back!"

Kofi could hear his mother's voice through the hallway. This was a horrible scenario for Kofi and his mother to be in and for the rest of the family.

A week went by, and it was time for Lance's funeral. Kofi was dreading it and tried to delay getting ready, but it was time to get it over with. Afia had to make arrangements and contact each family member on her own. The funeral Director and embalmer did a great job on Lance by restoring his natural appearance. There were a lot of people at the church for the viewing before the service started.

When it was time for the service to start, Kofi and Afia waited until everybody got to say their goodbyes before they walked up to his casket. Afia had her arm around Kofi. He stared at his father, who was now just a vessel that transitioned out of existence. They appreciate everybody who came to show respect, but Kofi felt himself about to go into a deep dive of depression, and he didn't know how long it was going to last. His father's death was going to be a test to him, and he was unaware of how this new chapter was going to play out.

When the funeral was over, everybody was on their way to the cemetery. The pastor spoke and let a dove loose. Kofi spaced out for a moment during the somber affair. He just stared at his father's coffin while it was going down into the grave, and the waterworks flowed again while taking heed that it was tough road for the living, so crying it out was only necessary.

After leaving the cemetary, Kofi told Afia he wasn't going to the repass. He kissed his mother on the cheek and gave out a few hugs to family members and friends. Jerrod walked with Kofi.

"You mind dropping me back off to the crib?" asked Kofi.

"Not at all. I got you, bro. Are you still going to the repass?"

"Nah, I can't do it. This was enough. I'ma change my clothes, and I'ma go somewhere."

Jerrod dropped Kofi off and left. Kofi undressed, put something comfortable on, and took a drive. He just wanted to be off the radar for a few hours to clear his head. He decided to go to the North Shore Beach. It was the most convenient and one of the quieter beaches in the Miami area. When he got out and started walking, he was the only one there, which was what he wanted. He had all the time in the world to take a walk down the boardwalk. He placed his hands in his pockets and wept. His heart took a stabbing.

Kofi knew he had a long journey ahead of him with his grief. What bothered him the most was that Lance wasn't going to be there to see him walk across the stage for graduation. Lance always encouraged his to be himself, never be a follower, learn how to manage money, be a protector and a leader, try his best, even through failure, and know who to trust. All those elements were things Kofi was going to keep with him. Sometimes, he would call his father's number, hoping he would answer when the phone rang. It was hard for him to sleep. He tossed and turned several nights and woke up trembling. Afia felt it was necessary to see a counselor for grieving.

Kofi missed school a couple days, but he eventually returned. He wasn't ready to be around anybody at the time. When returned, Kofi was overwhelmed by the condolences he was receiving, even though he appreciated it. A lot of teachers told him it was fine if he wanted to leave early, but his pride refused to do so. He could be hard as nails sometimes, but he had to keep himself busy before he drove himself crazy. He tried his hardest to push his feelings to the back of his mind, but that failed to work.

Afia heard a knock at the door, and it was Jerrod. "Hi. Ms. Afia."

Afia let him in. "Hi, sweetie. Come on in."

"Are you doing okay? I just wanted to check in." Jerrod showed his compassion.

"I'm doing the best I can, Jerrod. Thank you for asking."

"Yes, ma'am. This is still crazy to process. There's nothing I can say to make it better, and I wouldn't wish this type of tragedy on anyone. I know you're deeply mourning, and I'm praying for peace. If there's anything you need, please don't hesitate to let me know, and that's also coming from my parents. You are family to us."

Jerrod knew Kofi was being distant as of late, and rightfully so. Jerrod made Afia's heart warm up by showing support.

"Thank you so much. Kofi is lucky to have a friend like you. The last two weeks have been hard and rough on him. He thought the world of his father."

"He treated me like a nephew. I love how cool him and Dad were. I'ma miss them talking about sports and how crazy their debates became," replied Jerrod as he reminisced.

Jerrod and Afia hugged, and she let him know that Kofi was upstairs, but she wasn't sure if he was asleep or not because it was quiet. "Go head and check on your friend. I'm sure he would love your words. He needs his spirits uplifted. I don't want him to suppress and numb his feelings away."

"Yes, ma'am. I'll see what I can do. I'll try my best." Jerrod went to check on Kofi. He knocked on his door while Kofi stared at the ceiling, thinking about life.

He turned his head when he heard the knock. "Who is it?"

"It's Jerrod, bro." Kofi was reluctant to answer. "Come on, man. Open up."

Kofi didn't say anything as he opened the door. He placed himself back on the bed.

"You know I had to come check out my nigga. I figured you wanted some space, so I gave it to you. How you feelin'?"

"I been dealing with my dad's murder. How you think I'm holding up?" screamed Kofi.

Jerrod wasn't the reason behind Kofi's anger. He stood by the dresser. "I know, man. You know I love you, bro. And there's no rationalization through the grieving stage." Jerrod felt compelled to say something to his friend. "I see I came at the wrong time. My bad, dawg."

Jerrod was on his way out, but Kofi stopped him. "Hold on, man."

Jerrod walked back to the room. "I can't pretend what would be in my head, or what I would do if one of my parents were taken away from me in such a violent act. I'ma always be here for you. That won't change. Til' the day I die." Kofi started crying again. "Let it out, bro. Don't have that shit bottled up. That shit'll drain you."

Kofi couldn't get vengeance even if he wanted to. There was no way of debt being paid.

"A part of me feels dead! How that fuck am I supposed to recover from this bullshit?" Kofi was frustrated and angry.

"The fact is you don't. At least not completely. You never will, because you're not gonna forget your pops. Every move you make, and everywhere you go, the big homie will be with you. You gotta keep living, bro," explained Jerrod. "I know it feels like life can be exhausting while we're alive and loved ones ain't here. We tend to feel empty handed, but we have a purpose."

Kofi stood up, and his eyes remained empty and dull. He put his head down and slumped his shoulders. "I just wanted to make him proud, and some sucka took my pops out and took himself out! That's some bitch ass shit. I wish I could kill that motherfucker for what he did to my dad!"

Jerrod patted his friend on the back. "Take it day by day, and don't be too hard on yourself. Let your heart piece itself back together, homie. On its own time, too. You feel me? You ain't on nobody's time but your own with this cycle." Jerrod was trying his best to convince his best friend that he needed to carry on Lance's virtue and to think about the great memories he shared with his father. "I'll leave on that note, bro. Call my jack if you need anything. Continue to live."

Chapter Eight
Infinite Landscape

I t was Kofi's first week at the animal vet clinic. Due to the unfortunate events with his father, Kofi had to push his start date back, but Nurse Hall understood the terrible circumstances at the time. He walked in and was immediately greeted by the receptionist.

"Good afternoon, ma'am. Do you remember me from a while back? I'm Kofi. I'm here to shadow Nurse Hall."

The receptionist recollected and told him that Hall would be over shortly to grab him up to show him the way. Nurse Hall walked down and guided him to back. He assisted with the kennels. He enjoyed being in an entry level position. During the shift, he took his iPad with him to take notes on the procedures that vets followed and asked plenty of questions, even when thinking he was bombarding. The nurses always respected when questions were asked. He volunteered to take one of the dogs out for a walk, and after he came back, he hydrated them and play with the rest of the animals.

"You're a natural, kid. I love to see it," said Hall.

"Thank you. I appreciate that a lot."

Kofi cleaned the cages. After he was finished, Hall was willing to show him how to properly find veins and count the medication because there was some downtime.

"What are the hours gonna be so I can lock in my schedule around other obligations I have?"

"We'll need at least three to four hours from you, and if you're fine with sacrificing weekends, we'd love that, too. If you can do every other weekend for the same hours. We recommend this for experience purposes, honey. There's plenty of students your age that are putting in countless hours, so my suggestion to you is to get as much time in as you can. Take advantage of it while you can. It'll only help you out in the long run."

"You got it," he replied. "Man... I can't wait to open my own clinic one day. Every time I'm in here, I dream about it more. This shit is dope," said Kofi as he cleared his throat from mistakenly cursing. "I'm sorry about that."

Hall ignored it. "You'll do well when it becomes your time. You're a fine young man, and you're a believer. I can see it in your eyes. Go head and get on outta here. Thank you for all you did today."

"It's my pleasure. I'll be back within a couple days."

The weekend was here, and Kofi was getting a tattoo portrait of his dad's face on his right arm. Lance's face on his son's arm was detailed. Kofi loved the ink on his skin. He also had Afia's name tatted on his neck. He was one of the very few in his class that had tattoos. Afia's name was his first tattoo. The tattoo aristo was finishing the lining and sprayed his arm and wiped it. Kofi got up and walked to the mirror to see the finishing touches on it.

"This is fire! Hell yeah! I love it."

Kofi received a text from Liviana after he sent a Cash App payment to the tattoo artist before he left. She wanted him to call her.

"Hey, Liv. What's up wit' you?"

"I wanted to see you. I haven't spoken to you in days, and I was thinking I may have did something wrong. I didn't see you at school, either. Were you avoiding me, shawty?"

"Nah, love. Not at all. I just been to myself as of lately. It wasn't personal against you. Been going through some tough ass times, that's all. I haven't had much rap toward anybody. Been lasered focused on me. What did you wanna do? You want me to come over?"

"I was thinkin' something simple like taking a walk," Liviana suggested.

"You can never go wrong with a nice walk. Where to?" Kofi asked.

"I found a spot, but since you're from here, you most likely already know where it's at, or at least heard of it."

"Oh yeah? Check you out doing your lil' research. What's it called?"

"It's nothing glamorous. I wanted to find a place that was quiet. "It called Morningside Park."

Kofi was impressed. "Hell yeah! That's a good ass park. When did you wanna slide over there?"

"I want to right now."

"Shit, I'm down. Do you want me pick you up?"

"Sure."

"Say less. I'll be on my way."

Morningside Park was one of those hidden gem environments that was known for its quietness. It was the perfect place to have picnics, paddle boarding, swimming, and plenty of other recreational activities with beautiful wildlife viewing. It also had a nice playground for children. What Kofi would soon come to realize was that Liviana loved the beauty of nature.

When Kofi pulled up on Liviana, she got in and noticed from her peripherals that there was a basket in the back of Kofi's car.

"What's that?" she asked.

"What does it look like? It's a nice day out. I figured we could have a picnic."

That was romantic and sweet to Liviana.

Kofi and Liviana arrived and entered a gate before going through the park. Once they went through, Kofi found a spot that wasn't dirty and placed a blanket on the grass where they had a good view of the water, skyline, and it was calm. There were a few people that were out there, but they mostly had the park to themselves.

"This was a good place you chose. You can hear your thoughts out here and be sane. We could've went kayaking. Maybe we can do that next time." Kofi took noticed of Liviana's eyes lighting up at the park when she saw people running, swimming, walking, and enjoying life.

"Thank you for doing this. I don't like being around a whole bunch of people all the time."

Kofi pointed to the water where he spotted a dolphin fin. A few more popped up to where the dolphins danced. There were also a lot of beautiful homes she took notice of and liked.

"It's surreal that me and my mom decided to move here. I understand it more now, even though I'm still home sick from time to time," she expressed. There was a couple that was meditating. "See that over there? That's something that I always felt like could've been beneficial to me."

"Meditation?"

"Yes. And not just because it looks therapeutic, but it looks like it could help with positive emotions," she replied.

"That's interesting. Break that down more on what you mean by that. I like where this conversation is going," Kofi urged.

"I just mean that we're always busy doing other shit in our lives that we don't ever stop to think about what's truly happening inside of our lives. You know? The past, present, and our future. Or where we see ourselves in ten years. It's just the reflection I think meditation provides. Not always reflecting on misfortunes but true happiness or finding out what exactly it is that makes you happy."

Kofi felt those words in his soul. He was diggin' Liviana's introspection. It wasn't only profound but sexy at the same time. "Deep ass shit. Maybe I should look into doing that myself, especially with everything that goes on in this head of mind, but I feel like there are two ways to look at it, because not only could you be looking for peace, but over-thinking also could bring on unwanted anxiety as well. Sometimes it can be detrimental to your mental health."

"Do you ever challenge your thoughts?" she asked.

"Not so much challenging my thoughts, but more just controlling them to have a good influence on my life and making sure my mind is actually clear from the bullshit. Losing my dad fucked me up. It wasn't like he was battling with an illness. He wasn't sick. He was murdered, as I'm sure you heard on the news or at school, but one thing that life has taught me as young as I am, is that I can't self-sabo-tage. I have to deal with those mental wounds. Last thing I should do is shut out those who give a fuck about me."

Liviana sat Indian style on the blanket. "What good food did you bring for us? My stomach is touching my back right now."

"I'm glad you asked. What we have here is a Ghanaian salad." Kofi slowly brought the plate out of the basket, and it smelled great. "We have everything healthy with this dish right here. This is one of my mom's favorites. Vegetables with sardines, pasta, eggs, and baked beans. You'll love it, trust me." Kofi grabbed a plastic fork and put the food on it to feed Liviana.

The first bite she took, she immediately fell in love. "Oh, my fucking God... This is amazing. Are you sure your mom isn't a chef? She can really put it together. You weren't lying when you said I would love it."

Kofi continued to feed her. "Facts. Any time you want food from the motherland, just let me know. My mom can make anything. And maybe one day you could have the pleasure of meeting her."

Liviana was surprised to hear that come from Kofi's mouth. "That's big."

"Yeah, but that's totally up to you. No type of pressure at all. I just meant from a friend's standpoint. I don't want to weird you out if it comes off like that. My mom is a vibe. Everybody loves her. She's the homie," Kofi explained.

"How many girls have actually been introduced to your parents?"

"I can honestly count on 1 hand the amount. You're different. I know it sounds like the same ass tune any nigga would say when he's talkin' to a new girl, but I mean that shit for real." Kofi felt what made Liviana stand out was that they had conversations that were real and genuine. "We're just normal people doing normal things. Not have it be some type of weird ceremonial act but just friendly interaction," he continued to explain, and Liviana understood his point.

"My problem is sometimes not being comfortable with being vulnerable. It comes from past traumatic events."

Liviana and Kofi were relatable with certain realities at that present time. Even though both of her parents were alive, she was living with her mom, and she was an only child. Kofi was too, but he now only had one living parent. They both understood the pressures their mothers were under of raising their kids on their own. Liviana's dad was unstable from his drug habit, and he was in rehab. Her mother wanted to move out of the state because of it. She resented her mom for wanting to be as far away from Liviana's dad as possible. She just wanted a better life with new goals and new opportunities.

Liviana went on to explain to Kofi how she was around a tough crowd and often times started seeking validation from older men for not having a stabler father figure in her life. It didn't reach older men to the point of pedophilia but dealing with guys that took advantage of her mental innocence for things she didn't understand. She had to work on how she communicated when she navigated through life.

"It's a terrible feeling when you feel inadequate, guilty, constantly asking yourself questions of why you're feeling unworthy or scared. You can get used to shutting people out, and it's a natural defense mechanism to not want to get close," she explained. "You want people to love you at your worst. My dad put my mom in debt. Not only that, but he would also beat her ass in front of me, and sometimes, I didn't even know how to try to defend her. I was so young, and I'm not able to process what was goin' on. I was scared to get involved in fear he would do something to me. Money that was supposed to be for the house, he would spend it and smoke it all away. He never raised his hand at me, though, which is good... all things considered."

Kofi believed that relationships parents had always had to set the tone for what was in store for their children's relationships when it came to what was acceptable and what wasn't. Kofi looked around momentarily. "I do think it's safe to say you turned out good, even with what you had to endure." His compliment made Liviana feel good. "Life would be so much easier if we actually had a template to follow when it comes to love and our relationship with our parents. Before my dad died, when my mom and him got a divorce, I admit I felt like I was losing hope on something I'd be dealing with myself when I got older. I had to train my mind that I can't look at what my parents went through with those lenses that it'll be destined to happen to me."

Kofi couldn't imagine the damage that was done when a father and daughter that weren't on the best of terms could lead to a female's stress level, increasing not only mentally, but physically. Most didn't take heed to that. Kofi, by this time, wanted to shift the moment. Liviana felt safe and appreciated inside Kofi's presence. They also shared a lot of the same beliefs and values from their conversations.

Neither one of them wanted the conversation to stop.

"Stand up," he ordered, shifting gears.

"Why?"

"Because I wanna show you something. Just come with me." Kofi held Liviana's hand and guided her to the direction of a palm tree garden he noticed.

"Stand right there for me," he ordered. He backed up a few feet and took his phone out.

"What are you doing?"

"You're looking too good. I wanna take a few pictures of you. This is a good angle. Trust me, I'm nice. Pose for me, and don't be scared, either." Liviana made a subtle pose and looked at the camera to smile. "Do another pose. Loosen up a lil' bit. Don't be lookin' all stiff. Do another." Kofi kneeled down on his right knee and turned his phone horizontally. "Come on, girl. I know you can do better than that. Make that smile brighter for your boy!"

He took five more pictures in five different positions. Kofi adored the way Liviana looked in them. Each picture he took, it made her features stand out. Her jawline kept his eyes following them when she posed. Liviana was showing off her prominent cheek bones when she smiled, and her dimple showed on her chin. She also had a pretty set of lips with pretty teeth. Her severe eyebrows were intimidating and gave her a mean look, even though she was the opposite of mean. With it being gorgeous outside, it was only right that Kofi seize the moment to show her off to his advantage. Liviana posed like a work of art.

"Those came out good. Thank you so much."

"Of course, they did. I'm a hell of a photographer low key. And you don't even need to add any filters to them, either. You're welcome." Kofi immediately sent the pictures to Liviana. "Natural beauty is the best beauty."

When the two sat back down, Liviana scrolled through them. Kofi had grapes in the basket that he started to eat. To be playful, he tossed a few at Liviana.

"Are you ready?" he asked as he tossed a grape in the air for her to catch.

They took turns catching the fruit, and she caught more than he did.

"You got lucky." Kofi laughed. While cleaning up the mess they made on the blanket, Liviana could feel Kofi inching closer to her. The temperature rose, and Kofi's face had a serious demeanor. Her body langue softened up. Kofi rubbed his lips together, as did Liviana, while he touched her hair. He placed his arms around her. They were leaning in closer to one another and paused while both thinking about kissing. Kofi was confident enough that he didn't have to ask permission for a kiss, so he went in for the kill, totally not wanting to wait to taste Liviana's lips. There closeness worked its magic. Kofi slipped his tongue in, making her giggle, but she enjoyed it. They lost themselves in that moment.

It was now the spring time during the month of May, and graduation was next month. Kofi and Liviana remained spending a lot of time together the last few months. He loved showing her around the city of Miami by taking her sightseeing. They even checked out a few NBA games. The biggest flex that Kofi impressed Liviana with was when he bought tickets of the Miami Heat against the Atlanta Hawks. She was astonished when he surprised her with the tickets. She would love going to Hawks games when she was in Georgia, and the fact that she shared a common interest of basketball with Kofi being a

Heat fan was great. They were able to have a fun rivalry amongst each other. He also took her to an Orlando Magic game. They'd watch movies and cuddle and text each other all night until one fell asleep, even if it was on a school night.

During the stages of dating, they were introduced to the mothers, who also eventually met. They gave their approval. Left and right, Kofi still had to curve females just to be around Liviana. He felt bad and noticed the ones he once had benefits with, they felt a disdain toward him, but it wasn't personally toward Liviana because she wasn't around at the time. Some girls felt that at the very least, he owed them a conversation. He admitted that boundaries were never set in stone, and he wouldn't know how to react when a girl was genuinely into him, not just having a session. Signals didn't get picked up. To him, he just knew she was the one he wanted to be with. It was a refreshing feeling for Kofi at his age. He was sampling everything moving because that was what a young man's priority list was and not being tied down. Kofi always chased his high since his infatuation was such an easy look for him, but it became apparent that Kofi and Liviana were comfortable, and there was no way around it. He shut himself away from the world because she was the only girl that mattered. That was when he decided that he wanted to make it official, but only if she was willing to accept his invitation.

On a Wednesday evening, Jerrod was seeing a girl, and he wanted Kofi to double date with him. Jerrod's idea was going miniature golfing, and it sounded like a plan. Kofi also had an idea of going bowling.

Kofi and Liviana walked inside the bowling alley where Kofi saw Jerrod landing a strike and then ordering food. He noticed Jerrod waved toward his direction. "We over here, bro! Come on so we can start a new game to get your ass kicked."

Jerrod's date name was Alyssa. It was her turn, but beforehand, Kofi introduced Jerrod and Liviana to each other.

"What's up, Liviana? Nice to finally meet you," said Jerrod politely. "I saw you a few times at school passing by. You got my nigga smiling ear to ear a lot lately. That's exactly the type of energy he needs right now."

"Nice to meet you, too. Kofi told me a lot about you."

"Have y'all made it official yet?"

Kofi tried to awkwardly change the subject. "Chill, bro. We're just friends."

"My bad. My bad," replied Jerrod jokingly.

Jerrod introduced Alyssa to Kofi and Liviana. She was quiet but friendly. They spent a couple hours bowling until Liviana was tired and ready to go.

Kofi dropped Liviana off back home. Before she was about to get out, he shut the car off. She noticed that Kofi seemed anxious and nervous.

"Are you good? You feelin' okay?"

Kofi sighed and turned to her direction. He grabbed a hold of her hand gently. "Listen... this is something that's been on my mind for months, and I can't even lie... it's been scary." Liviana was bracing herself. "You became one of my closet friends since we've been spending as much time together. I wanted to ask your opinion on how you felt if we take things to the next level. I'm not saying we have to rush into marriage or anything crazy like that, but I know for a fact I wanna be with you," he explained. "I want this to be exclusive. You're not like these other chicks. You carry yourself in a different light. I rather risk going through hurdles and pitfalls with one chick who really has my best interest at heart, sees me for me, and risk it not working out."

After pouring his heart out, Liviana stood silent

for a moment, and that worried him. Kofi was wondering if she had anything to say. He was giddy and terrified all in one. He noticed Liviana looking away out the window. Now, Kofi felt that maybe they weren't on the same page as he might've thought. He was riddled in confusion. "Damn... I just said a lot, but I guess potential titles push you away."

Kofi was being sarcastic.

"You're way too hard on yourself," she replied with the biggest grin on her face. That was when Kofi realized she was joking around with him. "I wouldn't have it any other way. I can say this with my heart and confidence that I've been falling for you," she replied nonchalantly. "I love how much you pay attention to detail. I love how we talk on the phone until we pass out. I love how you're confident when you talk about things you love to do or are willing to do in the future," she explained. "Every single day with you feels like you've been around me my whole life, but just so we're clear, I want consistency. I'm fully aware of your reputation out here, and I'm not coming second to no bitch." Liviana wanted to make sure she was crystal clear. "And I mean it."

Kofi got out and opened the car door to let her

out, and he immediately brought her closer to him and locked his arms around her waist. "As long as this relationship runs its natural course, I feel we can keep each other on our toes. You have dreams just like I do. I don't wanna be around anybody else emotionally and physically. I'm not on no bullshit. I'm here for any bad times and rough patches we may have along the way, but one thing for sure is I want you. And worst case scenario, if it doesn't work out, we can always remain friends. I'm cool regardless." Kofi playfully kissed Liviana on her nose and brought her closer again for a strong hug. "I'm falling for you, too."

Afia and Kofi were at the nail salon. That was another place they'd go to bond and relax. They were both getting pedicures. With Kofi being an athlete, he always kept up with his maintenance. He was listening to music. Afia tapped his shoulder to talk to him when she saw the was smiling at his phone. Kofi turned to his mom when she got his attention.

"Somebody is happy over there."

"I am."

"What about?"

"I told Liviana I wanted to be together exclusively, and she was down!" Kofi was excited.

"I already thought that you two were together, considering how much you been raving about her and hanging out. As long as you're treating each other well, I have no qualms. You'll continue to have my support and blessings, baby."

Kofi felt like the luckiest nigga in the world. "No doubt. I appreciate that, Mom. For real. Thank you! It's hard to believe sometimes how connected you feel toward someone. As many girls that I've been around and entertained giving my heart to, they haven't got close to what Liviana has to offer."

Kofi officially applied at the University of Florida, like he always planned to, and was waiting to receive his letter in the mail. His grade point average remained one of the best in the school, with over a

4.0 GPA. He took the ACT and the SAT, scoring high on both.

Afia and Kofi walked inside the house, but she walked back outside. "Shit. I forgot to go to the mailbox. I'll be right back."

When walking back inside and looking through each piece of mail, she noticed the University of Florida envelope with Kofi's name on it.

"Kofi!" yelled Afia. Afia had the envelope in her hand. She placed it on the table. When he came to the kitchen, she picked it back up and handed to it him. "Look, baby. Check this out. Let's see what it says." Kofi let out a deep breathe, bracing himself but hesitated to open the letter. "What are you waiting for?"

"I can't even lie... I'm nervous about this. What if they didn't like the essay I wrote to them about my academics and why I'm a good applicant?" Kofi started sweating. He ripped open a piece of the envelope and stopped.

"You have no reason to be. I raised a young man with a great personality. You did everything you could to showcase your skills, baby. Go ahead and open that damn letter."

Kofi shrugged his shoulders. "Okay. Let's find out." Kofi ripped open the envelope. He read a couple lines and realized he got in. Kofi threw the paper in the air with excitement. "I've been accept-ed!" he screamed aw the top of his lungs as he danced and stomped.

"That's what I'm talkin' 'bout, baby!" Afia clapped. Even with Florida not having a high accep-tance rate, there was no denying Kofi because his profile was too strong to pass up on. Not only because of his grades, but the work he put in through extracurricular activities and test scores. It was inevitable.

"Will you be able to handle me being five hours away?" Kofi instantly thought about how it was going to be too far.

"This is an opportunity for you, and I'm not getting in the way of that at all. I will be fine," answered Afia. She pinched his cheeks. "I am so proud of you, baby."

She cried tears of joy.

"Now I gotta talk to Liviana and see what the plan will be. This'll be fun." Kofi was worried about the future of the two because they just got together, and everything was going well. "I'ma have to call her. Things been runnin' smooth. I need to handle this sooner than later."

Kofi called Liviana to see if she was home, and

she was. He headed over there to speak with her in person. He was thinking they were gonna have to end fast as hell because of him being far away. His mind was racing with sadness and anxiety of what the outcome would be and if this was good news or not.

Liviana stepped outside and stood on the porch while she watched Kofi walk up. He cut right to it.

"I just got accepted to the University of Florida. You know that was my number one option since the beginning." Kofi couldn't hide his anxiety if he wanted to. He immediately got lightheaded and felt like his brain was attacking him while looking at Liviana. He was right when stating that she knew ahead of time what college Kofi was banking on, but unbeknownst to him, Liviana applied to the University of Florida as well, because she already planned on sticking by his side, and her course of study was there.

"I was actually on my way over to your house before you called me." Kofi closed his eyes and turned away from Liviana with self-doubt as he tainted with pessimism. "Babe, why are you acting like that?" Liviana pulled a paper out from her back pocket and handed to Kofi when she told him to turn back around. He read it, and her eyes were watering, but he didn't notice because he was reading.

"You got in to the same college? Oh shit!" Kofi let out a breath of relief and held his chest. Liviana smile while wiping her tears.

"Yes!" The two embraced each other tightly.

"This is big news. Hell yeah! Did you finally figure out what you're studying for?"

"Yes, I did. I'm getting my degree in Business Administration. It may not sound like the best, but it'll get me to the next step. I know it'll take me places." Liviana also knew it was possible that her course of study could've changed if she wanted it to. It was common that students jumped from different fields all the time.

"Don't downplay yourself. A degree is a degree at the end of the day, and it'll be valuable. I believe in you... Shawty!"

"That was cute, and that means a lot that you believe in my ability. I want to meet a lot of people in the industry of real estate a couple years from now. I wanna rub shoulders with clients and make solid transactions, even if I don't make the amount of money I want to right away. Whatever is destined for me, I know it'll pay off in the long haul. Will you be by my side?"

"That's not even a question," replied Kofi. "I can't have it any other way. And neither one of us need be an instant success story, but we'll be on our way. I don't care if we struggle. We'll find our way regardless. I couldn't care less about risking the failure when I know nothing comes without effort." Kofi could tell that Liviana had a competitive spirit, even if she didn't show it much. She had the fire in her eyes and willingness to be great.

"I love it."

It was the day of graduation. Kofi looked at Liviana with her cap and gown on. Her hair was straightened, and her makeup was done well. When walking up to each other, they kissed, and they locked their pinkies together before unlocking them to go sit down in their designated areas for the graduation ceremony.

After their classes names were called and they received their diplomas, the class threw their caps in the air with Jerrod leading the pack in doing so, leaving the teachers clapping. They went around signing year books and taking pictures with class-mates. Jerrod came over to take a few pictures with Kofi, and they made a few videos for social media.

"We finally did it!" yelled Jerrod.

"Let's go! Nigga, we made it!" Kofi yelled as he started to giddy.

Liviana laughed. Families were talking. Kofi was just happy as hell about finishing school. Walking across that stage was one of the best feelings ever. It was up.

"Bro, it's only right that we celebrate tonight!"

Kofi was down, but he had a different plan beforehand. Three weeks prior, he bought a ring because he planned on proposing to Liviana. "I'm down, but I have to do something before I step out. I got you though, nigga. We finally free!"

"Yessir! And then it's time to pursue our dreams! Go head, bro, and do what you gotta do. Just hit my phone later. I'm definetly getting' twisted tonight for sure."

Kofi laughed. "What else is new? You already know, bro. Be careful. Don't get too turnt before you forget what happened."

While walking to the parking lot from the expo center, Kofi asked Liviana if she could follow him to the car because he wanted to talk to her in private.

"We'll be right back," said Kofi as both their parents talked with the rest of the family. Kofi didn't do any talking once him and Liviana were secluded for the time being.

"What are you doing?" asked Liviana as Kofi kneeled on one knee. Kofi pulled out a diamond ring. Liviana covered his face. "Oh, my God. This isn't happening to me right now. Kofi, are you serious right now? You better not be playin' with me. This isn't funny. Does your mom know about this?"

"I'm dead ass serious. Liviana, will you marry me? And no, my mom doesn't know I'm proposing. I've been planning this for a long time." Kofi knew it wasn't the most intimate and appropriate setting to ask her that type of question, but he had to get it off his chest. He wanted Liviana to revel in her success, but he didn't want to wait another minute.

Liviana put both her hands onto Kofi's face. "I want to be with you. Yes, we just graduated. We put a lot of hard work in, and I trust you, but most of all, I love you. Yes, I will marry you, Kofi!"

"I'm sorry, babe. You should be basking in your achievements, and here I go with the extra pressure and shit. I'm trippin' right now."

"You're fine. I know it took a lot of courage for you to do this." Liviana assured Kofi that she wasn't uncomfortable and that she didn't agree to marry him because she was uncomfortable and didn't want to upset him but that she could see herself lasting a lifetime with him.

"You, as my future wife, have to be a reflection of me. I want you to look at me as a leader, and I promise I will protect you. I want you to follow me." Kofi wanted to be respected and controlling the pace of their relationship while she set the peace in the relationship.

Liviana understood, and she thought it was an even exchange. "You're not worried about us going into this fast right after we just graduated?"

Kofi shook his head. "I'm with you. Since my dad's passing, I wanna keep my people closets to me always. I'm not shying away from that. I'll take my chances."

Earlier, Liviana's mother gave her a note from her father that congratulated her on her graduation and wished he was there but had to get right internally and was hoping to have a better relationship with his daughter once he got completely sober. He wanted to do the right things to stay in her life. He wasn't allowed to leave the state at the time. She appreciated all his kind words inside the letter, and it made her feel good, even though she wished he was front row center to see her walk across that stage. It was heartbreaking, but she kept her head held high and had Kofi by her side to keep her going. They told the mothers about the proposal. Kofi stood tall to Liviana's mother and asked if he had her blessing to marry her daughter. Liviana's mother's face was giving off worried, as did Afia's, but Kofi and Liviana were going to do what they wanted regardless of the answer. Both were good kids, and they saw the good affects they had on each other, so they weren't standing in the way of that.

Kofi walked Liviana back to her car.

"I can't believe I have a fiancé," said Liviana. She couldn't stop kissing Kofi.

"I know, right? I can't wait to tell Jerrod later."

At first, Liviana wanted Kofi to keep the marriage between each other, but she changed her mind once she saw how excited Kofi was so show her off like he always did.

"Listen, babe, before you go, I don't wanna keep you any longer, but I wanna get this off my chest."

"Yes?"

"I know this is a lot, but I wanna break this down for you so you understand. I want you to be able to protect yourself when I'm not around. Not fold under pressure. Not downplay yourself or what you're capable of. While we focus on this next chapter in our lives, I guarantee you will tap into your fullest potential. That's the best jewelry in the world. It's bigger than this rock on your finger that I just placed on you," Kofi explained. "And yeah, we young, and we both have our faults, but once we get married, you can't just be in love with me, you gotta be completely sure you truly love me. I know you have a good heart and want to do good things, and you will for sure do those good things with me by your side. I wanna be able to feel comfortable talking to about anything, whether it's positive or negative. If I'm having a problem, I'd like to know I have a listening ear who genuinely cares about what I'm going through. And if I fuck something up, I'd still like to feel loved despite your disapproval, and if you have to criticize me for anything, I'd prefer your criticism be constructive."

Liviana nodded her head. "You already know, babe. As far as me... I wanna know that you trust my sentiments when we cross that bridge. We gotta continue to think and talk about what motivates us. This'll be a challenge."

Kofi agreed. "For sure. For sure. All we need to do

is elevate each other's spirits, and we'll be fine. Hop on this journey with me and conquer the world, my future Mrs. Dixon."

Kofi stuck his hand out to grab Liviana's hand. He gently kissed it, showing his admiration, respect, and sincerity for her.

Act Two

Chapter Nine
New Beginnings

Fifteen years later was a hell of a transition in time. Kofi and Liviana both graduated from the University of Florida. He applied everything he learned in college to his career. The couple both got their bachelor's Degrees. Liviana got her degree in business administration, and Kofi got his Doctor of Veterinary Medicine. He excelled in prerequisite courses. Before Kofi came along, it was hardly a thought in the back of Liviana's mind that she wanted to attend college. Her moving to Miami was a blessing in a disguise, like Kofi told her years ago.

Both were close to their mid-thirties. After college was finished, they decided it was time to get married. Jerrod, of course, was the best man. Before they became established, Afia didn't think it was a good idea that they got married as fast as they did. Neither did Liviana's mother, for that matter, but they had to take a back seat. They were old enough to make their own decisions. Kofi was ready to tie the knot with his fiancée, and he did just that.

Some days were worse than other days financially, but they had the plan to get regular nine to fives to save up tons of money before they bought their home. Kofi and Liviana's mothers were close enough and established a good rapport enough that after college, Afia didn't mind if Liviana stayed with them until they could afford to finally be on their own. They focused on building their credit. Both were intelligent enough to be able to handle expenses while also putting in a good percentage into their 401k account.

There were times where Kofi was completely off the radar when Jerrod was trying to get ahold of him to hang out. Kofi had bigger things he wanted to put in play to ensure plan and future was mapped out correctly. He prioritized financial security in their marriage. He made her comfortable that he was going to provide, and he took pleasure and pride in.

The couple was fortunate because their college career was counted as work history, so they were able to create leverage to the lenders for a home.

Kofi's business plan made sense, and once he was on his feet, he was guided to the resources to hire a lawyer, contractor, and architect to set up building his own clinical practice. He was able to get approved for a loan fast. With being Hall's protégé when he was younger, she was able to mentor him, and he remembered how much she would dig in his head to dive into books for researching so he would know about income. She told him she would've been willing to give him her practice when she retired, but he wanted his own practice, because grindin' to get it from the ground up felt like a different victory, and he didn't want to wait until she retired. He was grateful for the opportunity.

As a boss, Kofi not only was reasonable, but he didn't have time for his staff members to be funny about anything on the job. He needed strong and dedicated workers, or they would be fired in a heartbeat. He learned to be hardcore and straight forward from Hall, but still have compassion and understanding for employees. The brand he built had a good reputation, and he planned on it staying that way for as long as he could.

On the flipside, Liviana was working on attacking the real estate market. The first thing she did was get hired on as an ISA. With how competitive it was being a realtor, going full fledge on her own wasn't beneficial, so she needed to be taught the game. She set out to be different. There were times it was hard to find buyers. She would rub shoulders with wealthy customers. There were many people around the world that had never been inside luxurious houses. She studied the communities and understood the market of homes the client was interested in. She hated her time being wasted. If clients didn't want to get pre-approved for their loan, it would piss her off. She respected when clients were on point and serious.

Liviana was in Orlando for an open house. She was waiting for a new married couple she met up with at her office several weeks prior from New York. Screening clients was essential before anything to make sure they could buy property, because having an open house for strangers was bad for business. Commission wasn't worth getting killed over if you didn't know who you were dealing with. It was sad the number of cases she read about realtors not being careful.

They were interested in a waterfront home because it was beneficial for health purposes. She wouldn't have minded living on the lake herself. She was waiting inside her car when the couple pulled up. She got out of her car, slaying like usual. She loved stepping in her power and making impactful decisions every time she walked out into the world. She gave herself a daily dose of inspiration. Liviana's job was to specialize in marketing. She couldn't settle for being average. She wanted to be the best and go the extra mile, so her clients would have faith in her. She knew her value as an agent, and she attacked different avenues.

"Hi, good afternoon," she said with a huge smile on her face. "Please, after you."

She guided the couple inside the home. The couple's names were Kevin and Stacey, and they were newlyweds. Their lawyer pulled up moments after, just in case they needed some help with understanding anything in the event they signed a deal. She opened the door and made a gesture for the couple to walk in. "I want to thank you guys for allowing me to assist you. Welcome to the sunshine state! I'm confident I can persuade you to do business with me."

"Thank you! We're glad to be here," replied Stacey.

"I know you guys are from New York. Florida is a beautiful state. I do have a question as we get started. When you hear the word *luxury*, what does it mean to you?" Liviana asked, picking the couple's brain.

While they were in the kitchen of the house, she offered the couple a glass of champagne. When they obliged to have a glass, she poured it for them.

"A pretty house." Stacey laughed.

"True, but it goes deeper than that. Luxury is about being comfortable and secure inside of your home. You pay for the quality. You define what your market is. It's important to figure out what exactly is important to you and what your budget is. The day in age that we live in, people want to upgrade from being surrounded by walls and a designated parking spot," Liviana explained. "It's all about overall living a good life. This home we're in right now is beautiful, and Orlando is beautiful. Unsure if you have kids, but in the event that you do or are planning on it, there's plenty of space when you're on the water. There are people who love to kayak or going on the boat to soak up the sun. The view is amazing!" Liviana went to explain to the couple that if they wanted to resell there home if they didn't want to stay, that waterfront property was a great investment, because the value went up. "This is a perfect asset for the both of you."

Liviana went on to show them the interior designs throughout the house.

"You want a house that has strong quality and durability, correct?" asked Liviana. The couple both said yes. "This is the right home for you, and the environment is friendly. I know most people when they think of luxury homes it's a price issue. Rarely do they ever take in account the amenities."

Liviana was told that Stacey was a cooker. She lived in the kitchen, so she needed a lot of counter space, which the house provided, along with a beautiful living room, and the ceilings were high. "And, sir, if you like cooking on the grill, you must take advantage of the backyard that's out there. The pool is great too."

The rest of the meeting, Liviana showed the couple the exterior doors, the garage, the number of windows, and the master bedroom. The couple was impressed. They loved the outdoor space and the garden, but most of all, they loved the privacy they could potentially have if they signed on. The couple had a real estate attorney that looked over all the paperwork, and he thought that it was legitimate.

"We will take it!" said Kevin.

"Great! Another toast, shall we?" asked Stacey.

"Oh, absolutely," said Liviana.

CLINK!

On the other side of town, Kofi was inside one of the rooms at his clinic. He had to put a dog down who was dying. He was making sure the family were taken care of and reassured them they were making the right decision, especially when there was no more quality of life. One of Kofi's workers got ready to do the procedure.

"Hi, family. I'm sorry you're in this position. It's one of the worse things our team has to do." Kofi was standing by the door handing out tissues to the family as their pet laid down with obvious discomfort. It no longer wanted to stand or sit.

"I'm not sure how many pets you may have had, but I'll go over how this works. First thing is first. You folks are doing the right thing. I know saying that doesn't mean anything, because we all here that at some point in our lives," Kofi explained. "Don't feel evil. If there was a way to prevent this, we would've tried. What we're doing now is giving the dog an overdose of anesthesia, but it'll be painless, and it will slowly stop his heart, hence putting it to sleep. I promise it'll be peaceful, and he's going with some dignity.

"I learned a long time ago as a kid when I wanted to sign up for this that none of us will ever truly get over that, but we sleep better at night knowing our friend lived an enriched life, and you were given immense joy. This is a better outlet than being in agony. Nobody wants to live like that."

Kofi made sure the dog was relaxed and put at ease. He was given two injections. The procedure was done, and before the injection was administered, the dog transitioned.

"You folks take all the time you need. There's no rush. You let me know how you want the body to be honored and what you prefer. It's totally up to you if you'd like to elect to take him back home. If you prefer cremation, then we can do that, and you can keep the ashes, but please allow several weeks to get it back to you," Kofi explained.

The clinic could be a mad house on certain days. Kofi walked out of the room and saw a woman with her cat in her arms because the cat was bitten. She was panicked and panted from fear because the wound was deep. He heard the commotion in the hallway. It happened no sooner than he was about to sit down but had his team guide her to a room.

Ten minutes a later, another woman walked in with her dog because it was getting spayed. She had an appointment set up. She was visibly flustered and feeling guilty. Women were emotional, so it didn't alarm Kofi, and he assured it'd go as planned. Kofi told the owner to come back in three hours before picking her dog back up.

After the procedure was done, Kofi came out with the anesthesiologist. Kofi was staring at the dog's owner. He pulled himself together from his daze and put the leash back on the dog and went to the lobby. "Excuse me, miss. Bella did a great job. She's a trooper. Just make sure she gets plenty of rest, understand? Her anxiety is up right now, so we gave her a shot for ease. She'll be whiny. Make sure you're looking at her incisions for leaking blood. She'll be irritable for several days, so be patient with her. She'll be fine," explained Kofi.

"Come here, baby," said the woman as she kneeled. She grabbed the leash from Kofi. "Thank you sincerely for taking care of my Bella."

"My pleasure. She's exhausted, but I'd say five days from now, she'll be back to her usual self and jumping around. Don't feel guilty about the procedure because you don't want to risk any future sickness. You saved money." Kofi suggested that she receive CBD treats and getting the dog a onesie. "The onesie will restrict Bella's movement. We can give one to you for no cost. We have plenty here at our practice. How does that sound?"

"Sounds great. Thank you."

"You're welcome. Enjoy the rest of your afternoon."

"Wait, excuse me,"

Kofi had his hands in his pocket and turned back around when he heard her voice. He walked up to her. "Yeah? Something else I can help you with, ma'am?"

The woman thought Kofi was fine. "I know this may be an inappropriate setting for this, but with all due respect, you are lookin' bomb."

Even though men were natural born hunters at heart, there was nothing wrong with a woman going after what she was interested in. Kofi couldn't tell if she was shooting her shot at him. They both sustained eye contact with one another as she initiated more conversation with him. Kofi cleared his throat from being caught off guard. He turned around to make sure his workers weren't paying attention and didn't hear their conversation.

"Thank you for the compliment." He stayed composed and professional. Kofi had his white coat on a rare occasion. He looked smooth with his khakis, dress shirt, and his bow tie, with a clean ass cut.

"You're welcome. Would you like my personal number? My other number is already on file in your system, but you should call or text me sometime." The woman flirted subtly as she lightly touched Kofi's shoulder after thanking him again for treating her dog.

He decoded the signals she was giving him. He lowered his voice and suggested they continued the conversation outside. He led the way, opening the door watching how she moved, and she was looking like a supermodel in regular clothes.

"I saw the way you were looking at me in the lobby," the woman said calmly as she placed her dog in her car.

"Excuse me? I'm not sure if I know what you're talkin' 'bout. I'm at work."

"You're a bad liar. You don't have to play it off. Don't get all weird, honey. I won't try to get you in trouble. I understand if you're not receptive to talk to strangers."

Kofi admitted that he was looking at the woman,

even though she already knew. "I guess I'm bad at disguising it. I'm sure you're aware of the society we live in now. Men can look at a woman the wrong way, and next thing you know, he's on a Netflix special with his name attached to a *Me Too* movement, and his life is over."

The woman couldn't agree more. "That's a fact, but you don't have to worry about that with me because that isn't what this is. My name is Selma."

"Hi, Selma, I'm—"

"I already know your name. Your clinic came up through recommendations. Mr. Kofi Dixon. You have a great profile on your page." Selma had great social skills, and she had game. She wasn't the entitled type and didn't mind putting in work when she had eyes on someone. Kofi understood women enough that only a confident woman with common sense could pull off approaching a man in the manner Selma did. She was throwing signs that she wanted him in hopes that he would oblige and initiate it from there. Kofi put too much high value on himself and didn't have to stalk a woman or say corny lines to attract.

"I appreciate a woman who's direct. I salute that. You clearly know the secret to life, and I'm flattered." Kofi had a serious demeaner, yet he had sophisticated vibes and was always well spoken since a teenager.

Selma typed her phone number in Kofi's phone. He grabbed his phone back with the hand that didn't show his ring finger. His player ways were cemented in him. "Listen, get your dog back home so she can rest. I need to get back. I have a business to run. I'm not setting a good example right now. Make sure to call if there's any changes or you need help."

At the Dixon house, Kofi was home, and Liviana was coming in the door.

"Hey, my love," she said.

"What's up, lady? Come over here and give daddy some love," he replied. Liviana's feet hurt from her heels. He walked in the hallway and took her jacket off for her and kissed her forehead. "I love when you give me sugar. How you feelin' today?"

Liviana just wanted to sit down before she started dinner. "It was really good. I'm just tired from driving. I made a sale today with a couple from

New York, so that was exciting! They closed a deal on a beautiful home."

Kofi clapped his hands. "Way to score more wins, baby."

"Absolutely. Other than that, I just managed a lot of paperwork. I know I'm ready for a vacation. Speaking of which, I wanted to take a trip to Atlanta."

"When?"

"Soon. You think we can make that happen? We work a lot, and we deserve to fall back. Plus, I wanna visit my family and friends. I'm tired of having to be on FaceTime with them instead of seeing them face to face."

"That shouldn't be a problem. Time management is the only thing that worries me because I worry about my staff. You know I run a whole clinic."

As successful as the married couple were, Kofi had a hard time managing his relationship and his career, and he would indirectly choose his career over the relationship. He loved his education and financial independence, because he was filled with a ferocious amount of ambition. Liviana dropped it, and the couple enjoyed the rest of their evening relaxing.

A couple of weeks later, Kofi worked seventy a week. He constantly was on call because he had to respond to emergencies if necessary, and that was outside of his regular scheduled work hours. Often, he and Liviana weren't each other. Their schedules were conflicting. They'd call each other when she was on the road traveling. She worked nights and weekends and tried her best to set her own schedule, but she was basically still a rookie in the business. She maintained a level head, even when she struggled to find clients. There was more to it than touring homes because she had to focus on being flexible and being a people person. Kofi was the consistent bread winner, but it came with a cost. His clinic had different hours than the usual, and he was open seven days a week. Kofi was working on being wealthy, and he didn't give a damn about what statistics showed.

Through the agency Liviana worked for, she was around other successful men and women who would invite her to functions. Kofi would stay behind, which made her feel low and unsupported. When he was home, he was on his laptop or on the phone. She couldn't stand when he was being a man of just a few words and was limited with conversations when she was talking about how her day went, unless it was about what was interesting to him.

Everyday coming home, it was same song. Neither would initiate sex or be as flirtatious as they used to be because complacency seemed to be killing any joy outside of their work environment. Kofi viewed his mind as being logical, where Liviana thought he would be harsh with his words with the intentions on hurting her feelings, which in turn made her exhausted and annoyed.

Liviana heard the garage door opening. Kofi was walking in after chillin' with Jerrod for a few hours.

"I thought we agreed that days we both had downtime we would take advantage of it and spend time together."

Kofi rolled his eyes. "I can't kick it with my guys?"

She clearly never heard the song by Tupac "Run Tha Streetz" because those were his sentiments. Kofi didn't really fall into a group but still moved sometimes like he wasn't married.

Chapter Ten
She Wants More

Liviana was on her way to the nail salon for a manicure and pedicure. She was getting ready for an upcoming photoshoot for branding for her career. She hated when she had to wait to get in the chair and it was jam packed. This was the first time she didn't have an appointment booked. Her usual nail technician wasn't in because she was on vacation. Liviana was annoyed while she sat down scrolling through her phone. A woman walked over and approached her before she was about to head out the door.

"Excuse me, miss? I can take you in."

"I was looking to get a manicure and a pedicure, but I see that my nail technician isn't here, so I can come back next week."

"I'm available. I just finished lacing another client. I know I'm not your usual nail technician, but I promise I'll get you right. Come with me," said the woman.

"No, it's fine, really," said Liviana. "I can just reschedule."

She remained unsure, even though she was badly due for one.

"That won't be necessary, and I mean that respectfully. My skills are top notch. Not to hype myself, but I'm really like that. And once I'm finished with your nails and toes, I promise your man will be eating off them." She laughed.

Liviana finally bought in and gave the woman a shot. "Okay, cool, but if it's not to my liking, I'm not paying. Is that a deal?"

"That's a deal, but that won't be the case. I got you. I just need a lil' bit of faith."

Liviana was persuaded. "Let's see what you can do." She walked over to the chair.

"Can I get you a drink?" the woman asked.

"No, thank you. I'm fine."

The woman turned the water on. Liviana instantly got excited once the water hit her toes. She got comfortable and put her favorite mode on the chair for a neck and back massage and closed her eyes momentarily. She chose what kind of service she wanted when the woman handed her the book.

"Excuse my manners. I'm sorry. I didn't introduce myself. My name is Selma."

"Wow. That's a pretty ass name. It's nice to meet you. My name is Liviana."

"That's a pretty name too, and likewise."

Liviana was looking out the window. Selma inspected her body language. "Not to get in your personal business, but you look stressed, or you might just be tired. I know we don't know each other, and we literally just met like thirty seconds ago, but is there anything you'd like to talk about? I don't mind if you need to vent."

Selma was great with her hands. She massaged Liviana's feet until her eyes rolled back. "Ahh... Yes, this is my type of energy. Your hands are so gentle. It makes me relaxed. I feel rejuvenated and refreshed. You are heaven sent for this."

"What's on your mind?"

"I mean, you know... regular woman things," she replied.

"Oh, I get it. You mean man problems?" Laughed Selma. "Because if you are, you're not lying about that." Selma saw the ring that was on Liviana's finger.

"Something like that. I just been feelin' like lately he hasn't been paying much attention to me. I feel like we haven't been in tune with one another. He has such a workaholic nature that it's not even funny. Don't get me wrong, I love that he goes hard for his passion, and I absolutely respect it, but sheesh, can a bitch have some time too? He acts like he can get away with these little attitudes with me because he knows I'll tolerate it."

"I'm sorry. Is it just the feeling of being second to work, or is it a trust issue thing?" Selma applied lotion while listening.

"I can't say I don't trust him, but what I will say is that our intimacy has been lackin'. He hasn't given a reason not to trust him. At least, to my knowledge he hasn't. It wasn't a thought to me that he would have eyes for someone else new. I think my biggest issue right now is feelin' inferior to him. That sounds bad, doesn't it?"

"I can't judge you, especially if those are your true feelings. Why would you feel inferior to your husband? Are you jealous of his success of some sort?"

Liviana thought hard about Selma's question. She was finishing her French pedicure set, and they looked amazing. Liviana wiggled them playfully and made a boomerang on Snapchat.

"I was sleepin' on your skills. You killed this, and you deserve a damn tip as well. Thank you so much!" said Liviana with delight.

"I told you I got you. You better start an Only-Fans and turn those beautiful feet into some money makers."

"You're onto something with that. I just might take that into consideration. But to answer your question... I don't know. I guess it's one of those situations where I'm painting a negative self-image of myself." Liviana realized she felt she didn't have her own identity. Though she was in real estate, she felt she was still only known as Kofi's wife and that her accomplishments were being overshadowed. She was championing Kofi, but the energy wasn't the same, even though Kofi showered her with praise, it wasn't to the magnitude of her liking.

"Nothing that a good conversation shouldn't take care of, right?" asked Selma.

"Possibly, but I don't want to upset him. Plus, he's always been the golden child that seemed to do no wrong," Liviana explained. "He was popular in high school, and he still is now. For instance, there are times where we can be out having dinner, and I'll notice the way he smiles at a waitress. It makes me feel a way, even though it could very well be that he's just being friendly. He could have any woman he wants. On the other end, I feel like sometimes I don't deserve such a good much and that he's growing tired of my ass. When I see the way he looks at other women, I think he knows them personally and has done shit with them. My job also feels like it's in a recession period, and I don't like it."

Liviana was having a good time, and Selma appreciated the honestly and respected the fact that Liviana opened up, even with them being strangers. Selma encouraged Liviana that she needed to work on herself and remain in control of her destiny. "There's nothing wrong with finding yourself if you feel that's what you have to do to be happy. How long have you been married?"

"We got engaged around 18 and finished college in our twenties. We've been together fifteen years since our senior year of high school, but we got married after we graduated college."

"Shout out to high school sweetheart love.

That's adorable. You don't see that happening that often anymore."

"You're right about that." Liviana put the sandals on that the salon provided. She made sure her polish was dried completely. Her manicure was French as well. She was on her way out the door after paying. "Selma you said it was, right?"

"Yes."

"Great. Thank you for being a great ear."

"No problem, but it doesn't have to end here. We should hang out sometime. Whenever you have free time available and you wanna have a girl's night out, hit me up. The city isn't ready when bad bitches link up. You seem like the type of woman I can vibe and have fun with."

Liviana didn't see it as a bad idea. Plus, she needed to make more friends, because she only dealt with affiliates through the real estate company she worked for, but most of the time, it was strictly business affairs only.

"What's your phone number so I can lock you in? I can add you on social media as well."

When Selma typed it in, Liviana called her right away. Another client was coming in for an appointment with Selma.

"I'll let you get back. I'll text you."

"Take care."

A week went by. Physical health was important, and that was one thing Liviana didn't play about just as much as her husband. She and Selma bonded through similar hobbies. Saturday afternoon, Liviana and Selma were at the gym. Selma's favorite exercise was the kettlebell glute exercise, and she loved to squat. She had small shoulders and solid wide hips for her natural frame. Liviana thought she had a BBL.

"Did you get work done?" asked Liviana.

Selma put in the work to maintain her body frame that most would consider just average. "Not at all. Too many get that shit done. This is all from the muscle, boo."

Liviana looked down at Selma's ass through her leggings and gazed at her bulky legs. Her quads and hamstrings were the perfect ratio. "Sheesh. Your muscular definition is impressive, mami."

"Thank you. Your body looks good, too."

Liviana had Oner Active leggings on, and Liviana

playfully tapped her ass cheeks. Both women laughed. She never used equipment and didn't use a bench, either. All she relied on were two dumbbells and herself to get the job done. Her growth was far from proportioned.

"Hard work and discipline," Selma responded.

They went on to hit the treadmill. They were trying to see who could outrun who. Since the beginning of their friendship, they were in friendly competition with each other, much like how Kofi and Jerrod were with each other.

"How long have you been in Miami? You from here?" asked Selma.

"No, I'm originally from Atlanta, Georgia. I moved here about ten years ago, but I always look back on it, and it was for the best at the time. No family here besides my husband. Of course, my mom and my husband's mom. I was young, so I didn't have say so. I love the weather and the people. Miami has taught me well. I plan on going to Atlanta to visit my family soon. It's just a matter planning it," Liviana explained. "Work gets in the way the minute I'm on the verge of planning a mini vacation. It frustrates me."

"What work do you do?"

"I'm a real estate agent."

"Seems like everybody is working in real estate. I know you have your hands full. I know it's a lot of pain when it comes to legitimate investors. Prime real estate is where it's at, so I can dig it. Do you have any kids?"

"That's a fact. It's a lot of bullshit across the board because you're picking up slack from other people's mistakes, and it falls on you, even if you had nothing to do with the shit. You gotta to be in sync with everybody's emotions. My time is valuable, so I'm constantly in predicaments where I'm bussin' my ass for months trying to sell a home, and my time gets wasted. It's a piss off. I don't get my money back or my time, unfortunately," explained Liviana. "It's just me and my husband. We actually did have a kid on the way, but I ended up having a miscarriage, so that tore me up. I didn't know if I could conceive again, and I was scared to risk losing another one, and he hasn't been ready. I think he's scared to take the chance again. I'm actually glad you asked me that because that's what I wanna talk to him about it."

Taking it hard from losing a child was an understatement for Liviana. It was too much psychological stress and hormonal outbreaks, and she respected her husband through that traumatic time because he cut her slack when her attitude wasn't up to par. Kofi refused counseling when Liviana suggested it to maintain his emotions.

"That makes me wanna cry," said Selma as she felt her eyes watering up. "I hate hearing those stories about couples losing their babies. Our bodies are fragile, and a lot of men don't understand what we go through. I'm not speaking for the whole species but some. I have love for the ones that try to put themselves in our shoes when we have a lil' one growing inside of us. Just body changes alone are a lot." Selma couldn't wait for the day she was a made a mother, but she wasn't in a rush.

Selma was thirty-five years old. She was two years older than Liviana and Kofi.

"Do you ever think about getting married?" Liviana was curious.

Selma was high maintenance and didn't deal with just anybody. "Sometimes I do, but it's more of a what if thing, you feel me? I might never get married. I'm comfortable with the way I'm living now. I do want kids of my own, but on the flip side of that, I'm loving life and living it the way I please," she answered proudly.

"Are you seeing anybody currently?"

It was years since she had a serious relationship.

Her goal was to play it safe, and she didn't care if a person was unavailable. She loved to have fun. "I'm bisexual. I'm single to do what I want. There is a man I'm dealin' with and definitely has my undivided attention for the time being. He's adventurous, smooth, and sexy as fuck. I be craving his contact." Liviana giggled. "Girl, I'm so serious. He always has me creamin'".

"I know that's the fuck right."

The women gave each other a high five.

"Plus, a lot of these bitches be out here fighting over dick, and I refuse for that to be me." Selma had the state of mind that sexuality and being married didn't matter when somebody was horny. Selma loved moving inside a careless world with zero complications and expectations. She didn't give a fuck who wanted to judge her. Deep down, she was just avoiding emotional intimacy, so she often put herself in risky positions.

"Other than being a nail technician, what else do you do? Do you have any other hobbies or goals you're reaching for?"

"I'm wherever the money is at. I'm an exotic dancer. I hate saying stripper. That sounds like a cheesy ass term."

Liviana loved Selma's charisma and unapologetic aura. With how she was built physically, she knew she was eating off her hustle and looking fine as fuck while doing. "Get it, baby."

"You already know. I love to dance. Majority of my money comes from that."

"Those dancers get busy on them poles! Maybe you can give me lessons. I thought about building one in my bedroom, so one day me and my husband can role play, and I can incorporate the pole."

That sounded like Selma's cup of tea. "You just say the word, and I'll put you under my wing and teach you some moves that'll have your man goin' crazy over you. It could bring y'all closer together."

"You're like Diamond from *The Player's Club*?"

Selma thought that was a good joke. "Nope. I always related more to Ronnie. She was more of my style. I love makin' a nigga assume the position. She carried it the way I would've carried it. Ronnie was crazy as hell, but I thrive. I love the power I have over men who lust over a woman that would never give them the time of day. It sounds petty as shit, I know." Selma loved being in control, even at the expense of being looked as just an object. "As long as I have my bankroll and my Bella, I sleep well at night. I wake up and do it all over again."

Liviana was confused. "Who is Bella?"

"My dog."

"Got you. My husband is a Vet."

"Really? I just got Bella fixed at the vet."

Liviana checked her phone at the time. She had to get home because she had an important virtual meeting with a client about a house. "We had a great workout session, but I have to hurry home because duty calls. Text me later."

Later that evening, Kofi and Liviana were sitting at the dinner table eating. It started off as a quiet dinner until Liviana wanted to break the silence. Kofi was quiet because it was a day he put a lot of animals down.

"Baby?"

Kofi looked up. "Yeah? What's up, baby? I'm sorry."

Liviana stumbled over her words. She wanted to talk about family but was afraid about how Kofi would react. "I just wanted to talk about our future if you didn't mind."

He placed his plate to the side. "What about our future? I'm all ears."

"I wanna know how you feel about having another kid again. I feel like it's been long enough since the loss of our first one. I'm ready to start our family again."

Kofi released a sigh of annoyance. He put his head down. He was feeling boxed in, and Liviana immediately could tell where this was headed. She was attempting a healthy conversation. He took a deep breath and remained silent.

"See, Kofi, this is what I mean. The way you're acting right now off something important to me is the reason I wanted you to do therapy with me. Instead, you wanna be an asshole. You get beside yourself each time I bring up our unborn child. Why do you constantly put your guard up when I wanna have a real conversation with you about what's important to me? Do you think you were the only one grieving over a lost child? You're selfish, and you're cold."

Kofi tried to get a word in but was shot down.

"Excuse me, sir, but I believe I was still talkin'." Kofi gripped his fork and bit his bottom lip. "When it comes to my job, you say the same tired shit over again. Your encouragement feels so forced and scripted like you're not engaging with your wife." Kofi stood up and placed his plate inside the sink and washed it. He turned back around when he heard Liviana suck her teeth. "Those dishes can wait. Once again, you're proving my point right now."

Kofi sighed to keep himself from imploding at his wife.

"What exactly do you want me to say, Liv? Our baby isn't here. I don't mean to sound heartless 'bout the shit, but there's nothing we can do about it."

"Oh really? Could've fooled me because I didn't see you share one single tear after the loss of our baby. It's like you purposely pushed it off to the side to act like it never existed. I want to start a family again. Why is that so hard to understand? Better yet, why is that wrong to want?"

It was apparent Kofi wasn't on the same time, and it blindsided Liviana.

"We're still young as hell, Liv. We ain't dying tomorrow. We'll be here. You know I love you, but that doesn't mean we have to rush and go back to trying. That's pressure, and that bothers me." Kofi believed there was a lot of unanswered questions. "Even if our baby made it to the world, what position would that have put you in? You wanted to be a stay at home mom?"

Liviana got up from the table. "I can see this conversation is going nowhere. Besides, you are baiting me into an argument, and you shoot me down."

Liviana didn't appreciate it, and Kof was currently living in comfortability. He looked at having a kid as a burden at that current stage of his life. His mindset changed from the time Liviana was pregnant in college.

"I'm not saying never. We have all the time in the world. You think I wanna be in a position where you'll nag me all day if I'm not handling my business as a man?"

"Yeah, but I'm ready to try again. I can squeeze in having another kid and be able to take time off. We can survive off one income."

Kofi wasn't hearing it. "What happens if we're in a position where our jobs suffer? We can't have it all without something suffering. We can't live in a fairytale land. To think shit is easy is just a myth, and I'm not being an asshole when I say that."

Liviana feared that Kofi kept a youthful mindset, and she wanted him to switch up his attitude. "I just want to make sure I'm a priority in your life, baby.

That's all," Liviana went on to explain. She wanted Kofi to see her value.

"You are, but I want your support and to feel like you respect me. We took vows, and we both agreed to stick it out until the end. Motivate me to move mountains out here, Liv. I don't think you understand the emotional load I take every day, on top of unexpected losses, all while risking my own damn health."

"You're being selfish."

"How am I being selfish? Is it because the world doesn't revolve around you, Liv? Did it ever occur to you that I have my own problems to deal with? I maintain this roof over our heads. You're acting like having kids is a box that needs to be checked off right away. Let's be for real. I try my best because I care about you, and this is why I say I need to time to come down after lifting a lot of weight. I need to keep my ass in check too, so that way when it's time to help you, I have the energy to do so." Kofi was trying to jam it in Liviana's mind that her having a career with real estate and with the market crashing they'd most likely would have to mainly focus on his career, which he wouldn't have much time for kids, and sometimes, his wife. "Shit has to mix well, and right now, it doesn't. I don't wanna be a chicken with its head cut off trying to be everywhere at once. Are you willin' to have a child pay consequences for poor choices right now? Hmm? I didn't think so."

Liviana walked away annoyed.

"Why are you walkin' away when I'm talkin' to you?" Kofi got up and made Liviana stop. "I spent years after we graduated bussin' my ass to recoup the damn cost of college and helping you as well. I get money, and I believe in myself, and now it's a problem because I don't want to try for another kid?"

The future looked like it was at stake, and Liviana was worried about where the marriage was headed and that it was hanging by a thread of hope. They didn't go anywhere. They didn't start a family yet, and Kofi had the dominant career. He was addicted to winning, and his frame of mind was love didn't deposit the fees.

"You don't have to be so mean."

"And you don't have to be such a cry baby."

"Just forget it. You're right about everything. I need some air." Liviana grabbed her car keys and left.

Liviana called Selma. "Hey, girl. Are you busy? Can I come over?"

"I'm free. I'm chillin' right now. Yes, come over."

"I'll be on my way in a bit."

Liviana thought she was on the verge of losing her career. With her being in real estate, as much as she loved it and it kept her afloat, it consumed her to the point where she didn't have time to take care of herself, and often, she would be emotionally unavailable. To her, it was probably a wakeup call to relax and try to be a mom while Kofi handled everything else. She still told herself that real estate was her calling, and she wasn't backing down. She worried that her field didn't match her life. Liviana was missing the man in Kofi that validated her, and as of lately, she was receiving that validation from Selma because she listened and gave advice.

When Selma let her in, her voice sounded tired and stressed.

"Come in, love. What's the problem?"

"It's my husband. I decided to talk to him again about officially starting our family, and it didn't go as planned," she explained. "Granted, he was direct on his stance. I respect it, but it still concerns me, especially since he's supposed to be my lifetime partner. Feels like he threw a dart at my heart. He doesn't think I'm being patient, but I believe I have been."

"Do you think you're being rational? You and his

future have to meet one another in some way. Honestly speaking, you can't change his mind right now."

"I love him, and I know I can't force anything on him. Maybe he doesn't see me as something long term, even though we're already married. Ugh... I've always devoted my time to him and respected him as a leader, but I'm just confused."

Selma put her arm over Liviana. "Listen, take a step back and regroup. No more talk about your husband, and no more talk about your work." Selma snatched Liviana's phone. "Give me that."

Liviana was caught off guard. "What are you doing?"

"You deserve a night out with no bullshit and no work emails. Put your phone on do not disturb, and come out with me."

Selma was planning a cocktail party with a few of her coworkers from the strip club, and she was inviting Liviana. Selma was the life of the party, and she was always surrounded by the most beautiful women across Miami. She had many friends that didn't hesitate to link up with her to create lasting memories, and they gave them a reason to get dressed and slay.

Selma introduced Liviana to her girlfriends. As

soon as they entered the bar, they went right to bathroom and took tons of selfies. They knew they were bad that night. They danced and made videos for their social media.

They didn't stay out too long, so after the bar, they went back to Selma's house to have a game night and karaoke night. Selma's personality was golden. Liviana played classic R&B and even hip-hop records, and Selma sang and performed them. She wasted no time grabbing the microphone to sing her ass off, and when a ratchet song came, she twerked.

"Fuck it up. Fuck it up! Aye!"

Two hours passed, and Selma's friends left. The only ones that remained were her and Liviana. She cleaned up around the place and lit a few candles around.

"I can help," she offered.

"Sit there. I got it. I hosted the party. Don't worry about it, love."

"Hell of a night tonight!" said Liviana. "I can't remember the last time since I had some fun. I haven't been out in so long because I've been devoted to my work. This drink has me feeling amazing, too. I better get my ass back home before my husband has a fit or worries where the hell I'm at."

Selma watched Liviana get up from the couch and stopped her in her tracks when she grabbed her keys from her pocket.

"You know you're welcome to stay here if you want if you're not comfortable with driving home. I much rather you stay." Selma could tell Liviana had more than a buzz, and it wasn't safe for her to drive.

"No. It's fine. I'll be good. I don't wanna impose. I overstayed my welcome as it is. I'm a lil' tired. I just need my bed."

Selma wasn't entertaining Liviana's modest behavior. "Don't be silly. You're not gettin' in a car accident on my watch. Keep your ass here. Let's lay on the couch and watch a movie until we crash. Unless you're tired," suggested Selma. "I'm sure your husband will understand. Just call him and let him know you're at one of your girlfriend's houses, and you're spending the night. I'll grab a blanket out of the closet for you."

Liviana texted Kofi that she would be home in a few hours. The women cuddled together on the couch.

"I love a good snuggle."

Liviana buried her face into Selma's chest. "I

enjoy being here with you. You're a good friend. Thank you for taking me out. I can be myself around you. Makes it better that we have a lot in common. And thank you for being a great listener. I don't like talkin' about my issues because I get paranoid and depressed."

Under the blanket, Liviana looked at Selma as her safe haven for that night. The scenery was just right, and she was glad Selma convinced her to stay over. Selma played in Liviana's hair gently and rubbed her legs. She was beginning to doze off. Liviana rubbed her eyes and moved her head up closer to Selma's face. Selma kissed Liviana and at first, Liviana didn't know how to react to the kiss because she didn't expect it.

"Oh, I'm sorry. I don't know what came over me," said Liviana.

"Do it again," said Liviana, and Selma quickly grabbed her face and pulled her closer.

Liviana felt like she was having an outer body experience because she found herself elegantly dancing her tongue with Selma's. They didn't stop as they got comfortable on the couch. The kiss was perfect harmony as they were creating a new taste with each other. Both were moaning together, speaking their own beautiful language. It was amazing how alcohol could fuel a person. Liviana was being seduced by Selma, and Selma wasn't a rookie at seducing women who were straight. Any way she could take advantage of a situation, she would. As the kisses went on and became more intense, warm, and inviting, Selma slowly reached for Liviana's hair and twisted it around her finger and grabbed her cheek. Liviana could feel her heart racing. Selma's lips were gentle and made Liviana's body tingle. She moaned sensually. She moved her body to get on top of Selma, and she took her shirt off. She unhooked Liviana's bra and gave her kisses across her neck and continued to slam her lips against Liviana's. The women broke the seal completely as the panties were taken off.

Both women were completely naked by this time, and instead of fuckin' up the momentum of heading to the bathroom, they stayed right on the couch. Liviana made sure she was comfortable. Selma touched the bridge of Liviana's nose and bent down to kiss her navel and lifted her legs up slowly.

"Are you ready for this?" asked Selma. "I'ma take care of you tonight."

Liviana's eyes were closed, and she covered her face being slightly unsure and fearful, but she trusted Selma. It was time for Liviana to explore her curiosity.

Liviana arched her back. "Yes... right there. Mmmm, yes. That's the spot."

She squirmed, moaned, and gasped. She grabbed the back of Selma's head as Selma hummed. She gave Liviana a vibrating sensation.

"You're having a blast down there." She forced Selma closer into her, grinding on her face. Liviana's eyes never opened until Selma stopped after a few seconds. "No, don't stop!"

She released a plethora of curse words while tilting her head back and begging for more. She covered her face. Her mouth was wide open, and she whimpered. Liviana could've killed Selma due to the death grip she had on her face. Nothing was around besides the clothes that laid on the couch for her to desperately clutch. Selma could sense that Liviana was ready to explode. She looked up again and saw Liviana's eyes moving involuntarily, and the sounds were unintelligible. "

I'm goin'... I'm goin'..." The moans shifted to complete silence. She released herself. S

The women switched positions, and Selma placed Liviana's face inside her Arcadia. She couldn't wait for Liviana to taste the sweet nectar on her lips. During the encounter, Liviana's insecurities were washed away, and she felt a boost of confidence and wasn't at all squeamish. Selma tasted like spring rain. She grabbed Liviana's ears and rubbed them in delight. Moments later, she was sucked into completion, where she left Liviana's tongue with the taste of apricots on it. The women fell asleep.

Kofi was doing his Sunday morning calisthenics inside the living room. The living room was spacious, and music was playing. Liviana walked in the door, and Kofi quickly got up. He was drenched in sweat and was shirtless.

"Wassup, baby? Good morning. 'Bout time you got home this morning. I was worried when you didn't answer my texts right away." Liviana looked as if she wasn't in the mood. "Are you tired? You had too much to drink?"

"You know I know my limits. I'm just sluggish. I just woke up," she answered.

"Got you. It was smart for you to just stay where you were at. You must've been twisted." Kofi saw

Liviana's social media posts, but Selma wasn't in any of the videos. He noticed all women that Liviana was with, and he assumed they were women that worked with her at the real estate agency. They were all gorgeous. "Glad you had fun."

"Yeah, it was a good time. We came back to the house after the bar, did karaoke, and then I got tired from the liquor and crashed the hell out."

"Why don't you go get some more rest? Unless you want me to make you something. You thirsty?"

"No, I'm fine, babe. I'll just head upstairs and do some more work."

Liviana reminded Kofi of himself with work always on her mind.

"You sure? It's Sunday, babe. You should just relax."

She wanted to get a head start on her obligations for next week. "You know how I am. If I can tackle a task, I will." Liviana yawned. "Plus, I need to freshen up."

Kofi finished his routine, and Liviana walked up the steps. When she got to the bedroom, she received a good morning text from Selma and told her she didn't know she left. Liviana responded quickly by replying with a good morning and apologized for not letting her know she was leaving because Selma looked peaceful while sleeping. Liviana thought about last night, and it kept replaying in her mind the way they touched each other. She thought she was going through an identity crisis from how far things went the previous night.

Chapter Eleven

Jaded

K ofi was at his office, and it was the last day of yet again a long ass week. He was stressed. As far as he was concerned, his work was done for the day, and he had his assistant takeover. Though he loved what he did every day, he would've been lying to himself if he never experienced days where his profession had him fucked up. He was doing paperwork and was already frustrated when clients were late for appointments and animals were suffering from being neglected. Thinking back on it in retrospect, he understood why some people switched their careers because the profession was demanding. Today was one of those challenges because with him loving animals that came to visit, animals sometimes didn't feel the same way. He found himself in situations where he was kicked, stung, bitten, but he still found purpose, even through aggravation and pissed off clients who would try to fuck it up for him. Occupational hazards were a bitch. He was savvy, but it didn't matter.

He didn't feel like going home. Plus, he and Liviana were still bumping heads at the time. Kofi told his team he was leaving for the day.

Kofi walked to his car and put his stuff inside. When he got inside, his mind wondered about Selma. She was one of the happy go lucky clients he wasn't used to seeing because others were a lot to handle. He considered calling her, just to be friendly to see if she would answer. Low key, since being married, he wanted to see if he still had had it.

Selma was in her living room with her robe on, she just got done rolling up a blunt full of *za* and began to smoke. As soon as she lit it, she blew the smoke out from her nose with the pressure from her lungs. She sat back and relaxed with the music on. Her phone rang.

"Hello?"

"Good afternoon, is this Selma? This is Kofi."

"Um, I'm sorry, but I don't recognize your name," Selma said.

"You came to my clinic when you brought your

dog in for the spay surgery. Is that ringing a bell to you?"

"Oh! Yes! Now I remember. Dr. Dixon. Hi, handsome. Thank you again for your services to my Bella. She's feeling a lot better. We appreciate it so much! You're great."

"Please, call me Kofi. It's not business hours for me anymore. And it's my pleasure. A satisfied customer is always a good win in my book," he replied. "You popped in my head a couple of minutes ago as I was leaving. I figured I give you a call and see what you were up to."

"Not much right now. I have work in a few hours, so I'm just lounging." Selma tossed her lighter on the table.

"I was thinking maybe we could possibly have dinner?"

"Hmm. How about you try harder to be convincing for me," she suggested. Kofi was entertaining it. Selma wanted to see how fly and slick Kofi could truly be to persuade her to have dinner with him. "I love a man with a good mouth piece on him."

"This is what we're doing?"

"Are you scared?"

"I can't even pretend to be scared. I can't live my life that way."

"Good, so show me how convincing you can be. Describe what your ideal night would be when a taking a woman out. Woo me."

This was right up Kofi's alley. "Not a problem. My ideal night for a dinner date for a woman as gorgeous as yourself... I'd take you to a nice water-front restaurant, eat some delicious food, while sipping mimosas, check out some beautiful artwork, while enjoying the view of Miami. A woman with your beauty deserves to be treated like royalty." Kofi invited Selma into his world. He wasn't trying to be the center of attention, but he wanted to prove he moved like a king, and he considered himself Grand rich and highly pleasing. Selma was digging Kofi's aura.

"Mhm, keep going," she urged. "What would you feed me?"

"Nothing but the best. Only the immaculate," he quickly answered. "I'd feed you something like Peru-viana cuisine, and then follow it up with a sweet dessert like chocolate leche cake with banana or some chich morada. I aim to please at all times, and if you want to, we can dance. Did I pass the test?" he asked.

"I can't even lie, you sure did."

"Good. I'll make the reservations. You just make sure you're ready once I give you the time and send me your location."

That was all Selma needed to hear. She had some time to spare before she went to work. She hung up the phone without saying anything, which was odd to Kofi, but he took it no way.

Seven in the evening hit, and Kofi was in the garage playing pool. Liviana was upstairs in the bedroom going over paperwork with her fellow realtors. Kofi had to be quick on his toes to get out of the house. He had to come up with a good excuse, especially since he was coming out drippy. Liviana would for sure asked questions. After he was done playing pool, he went upstairs to get in the shower.

Liviana was on locked in on her laptop. She was typing, and she was surrounded by paperwork. She was in a slump with her job. She was barely making forty thousand a year. Kofi was her backbone, but she wanted the cash flow. Her success was gonna be determined through who she knew, and unfortunately for her, she didn't know any rich people to rub shoulders with to get her over the hump.

She sat Indian style, and she didn't budge until she smelled Kofi's Bond No. 9 Lafayette Street cologne.

"Where are you going?" she asked.

Kofi told Liviana that he, Jerrod, and a few others were headed to the Tea Room. "Bout to slide out with the fellas. What's wrong? You look upset."

She tapped her head with a few papers. "It's just a lot going on, and it's hard to manage time. I wish I had time to myself like you always seem to find," she replied.

"What's the problem now, Liv?"

"A lot of financial shit. I haven't completed any sales since the couple from New York. Like I said, it's hard to manage my time, and you know it's a lot of competition in Miami, and I haven't been sleeping the greatest. My phone constantly rings. I just feel on my own. I need to find different methods to keep making this network build. I have several buyers that were about to do deals, and then something came up and loans had been denied. I don't have time for the run around bullshit with people who aren't ready to do business. It pisses me the fuck off. They'll either just buy a new car or quit a job, and I just wasted my fuckin' time. I'm just annoyed. And you're always going somewhere."

"Is there anything I can do?"

Liviana moved her eyes up to Kofi. "No, not really." Kofi was trying to be a listening ear. "It's only temporary. I'll continue to handle business on my own. It's just a little bump along the way. I know I can do this. I just have to have more self-motivation and not lose sight of my entrepreneurial mindset. I need to work on making more friends and earn their trust."

Kofi folded his arm stood in front the door. "Just to give you a perspective. You've been doing this for years. Most people don't even last in the line of work for as long as you. That alone proves you have what it takes, baby. Work smarter and not harder. Be relentless" Kofi walked over the side of the bed and kissed Liviana on the forehead. "I'll be back in a couple hours." Liviana had a lack of a response as typed on her laptop. "I'll see you later. I love you."

"Love you, too."

Kofi recognized it was a weird exchange and that the *I love you* was dry. He just ignored it and went out to enjoy the rest of the evening. He shot Selma a text to be ready and to make sure she dressed amazing for the occasion. After texting Selma, he called Jerrod.

"Yo, bro!"

"What's up?"

"I know you're at the crib right now, but I told Liviana I was with you tonight. If she happens to hit you for whatever reason, make sure you validate that for me."

Jerrod knew what time it was, and he didn't ask any questions. He just went with it in a form of enabling. "Say no more. I got you."

"My nigga," he said as he hung up.

By that time, Kofi was already driving on his way to pick Selma up. She saw him pulling up, and she came out with a corset belt long-sleeve rib mini dress from Tom Ford with heels on. Selma was of Puerto Rican and African American descent. She was a great blend. She looked scrumptious. Looking like something to eat was an understatement. She opened the door and placed her leg inside, showing her long and shiny legs she had oiled up. Her toes were long with black polish. She caught Kofi looking at them. She executed her outfit perfectly. Her long leather black hair complimented the style with her skin tone. She also had the Tom Ford Fabulous perfume, completing her look for the night.

"You're looking phenomenal," said Kofi as his foot was on the gas. He pressed down while the car was parked from being distracted. He was embarrassed and put his head on the steering wheel, but it made Selma laugh.

Kofi and Selma pulled up to La Mar by Gaston Acurio, which was a South American restaurant. It was considered one of the best restaurants in the whole city of Miami. Kofi paid for valet parking. His car wasn't the only car that was luxurious. All types of cars, from Mazaradis, Lamborghinis, and Bentley's, were in the parking lot. Everybody was going to the same restaurant. It was popular for its romantic atmosphere. Kofi walked over to the passenger side and let Selma out of the car like the gentleman he always was.

Kofi made sure that they had the perfect view. Kofi pulled Selma's chair out, and she sat down. "Thank you."

The waiter came up as they were looking at the menus. They started off with cocktails before ordering their food. "This view is top notch. I love this."

"I'm glad you do," Kofi replied.

The music wasn't too loud, so everybody was able to enjoy their food with no problems, and the DJ was playing smooth jams to set the tone of the night. Selma was still looking for what seemed appetizing to her while Kofi already knew what he wanted. They finally ordered, and it didn't take long for their food to come.

"I'm surprised that you were able to make reservations the same day."

"Yeah, I'm surprised myself, but I'm glad."

Selma took a bite of her food, and she melted from how amazing it tasted. "How long have you been at your clinic?"

"For about five years. It's been a long ass road, I'll tell you that much."

"How fulfilling is it?"

"I think it's real fulfilling. I didn't think I'd be in the position I was in now with having my own practice. It was a lot of money," explained Kofi. "One thing I learned is that I have to invest in myself at all times. I grinded to be in a position where I'm living great and doing what I love. Luckily, I didn't have to start from scratch, and I was able to convert a building that was already there."

Selma was respected the grind. "Sounds like you've always had a good head on your shoulders. Business seems to be boomin' for you. When I walked in, it was busy as hell. It looks hectic."

"I appreciate that, and not to toot my own horn,

but you're right about me having a good head on my shoulders, and I always had the drive. I don't bullshit. I care about my brand and my reputation. If my team doesn't give the clients the best possible care, then that means we fucked up. Plus, I don't overcharge my clients. I'm gentle with everybody."

Selma could tell Kofi showed a lot of dedication, and she was able to read off a plethora of characteristics she saw in him. She could tell he was passionate and put a lot into communication. The attraction was already built.

Kofi initiated eye contact on Selma. He didn't waste time transitioning their conversation. He knew when to stop talking, and he was ready to listen. "I think I said enough since we been here. Tell me about you. What's your line of work?" he asked.

When Selma spoke, Kofi directed his eyes at her pretty lips. "I'm a nail technician. I'm currently working on trying to open my own business one day. It's a competitive field, but I love working in the beauty industry," she answered.

"I can see you really thriving in that, and even though you're in a competitive field, I'm sure it's always profitable. Do you work at a shop?"

"Yes, I have work under someone else, but I'm building my clientele. It used to be a hobby, but then

I started practicing on people, and they encouraged me to take it seriously and make a profit. Matter fact, I just worked on someone new. She didn't trust that I was as good as I said, but I hooked her up, and she was impressed."

While Selma was explaining, there were moments she got nervous because Kofi remained focused on her eyes without looking away. She felt dominated, but Kofi was fixated on the sound of Selma's voice and the sound of her words. She paused for a moment and lost her train of thought, fumbling on her words, but she recovered. Kofi couldn't help but have a high degree of focus on Selma, she had his undivided attention.

"You're a good listener." Selma didn't tell Kofi that she also was a dancer at Gentleman's bar for extra income. Most of her clientele were with the strippers, so her customer base skyrocketed

While Kofi and Selma were conversing and enjoying their dinner, Selma randomly made a subconscious glanced down on Kofi's fresh mani-cured nails while he was putting his glass down. She noticed the ring on the finger.

"Why didn't you tell me you were married?" Selma was curious as to how Kofi would respond, because there was no way to ignore her question.

"I'm just confused on how you could just gloss over that. You're here with me, but you have a wife at home." Kofi sat his plate and glass to the side and folded his hands together. "Or are you gonna refuse to answer me?"

"If I admit to you now, does that change anything?" Selma was stuck for the moment. "I think it's a little too late for that. You know you don't want to leave, and I don't want you to leave. We're having a good time. At this point, I don't see how it's relevant. I just took you to dinner, and I never said I wanted anything from you." Kofi took a sip of his champagne. "You can do whatever is you wanna do. You're single. Was I supposed to lay all the cards out on the table for you?"

"You have a point. Well played. I guess I'll be the villain if I take you away from your wife and borrow you from time to time." Laughed Selma. "You're playing a dangerous game. I just hope you know that, but I'm here for it."

Selma knew dealing with somebody who was married was a dead situation. She didn't give a fuck if there was no future if she was getting what she wanted, and it was consistent. She always had options, and she played the game well. She was the definition of a bad bitch across the board. The fact that Kofi had a wife wasn't gonna end the spark between him and Selma. The presence of his ring didn't change her interest.

"Are you ready to go?"

"Yes."

Kofi drove Selma back home. When he pulled up to her condo, he stopped her before she got out of his car. "I hope this won't be the last time I see you."

"That's so sweet. You're already attached," said Selma sarcastically.

"Any man would be attached off rip if he's in the presence of you. You can't blame me for that." The way Kofi and Selma would engage, sparks were constantly flying. He couldn't stop gazing at her perfect oval face and being mesmerized by her clear skin and large eyes. "Call me anytime. I'm always available."

Five Days later, Selma called Kofi's phone while he was in his home office at his house. Liviana never disturbed him when he was in there, because if he was in there, he was working. He loved peace and quiet with a great workspace, and there was more flexibility for him to be in his own domain.

"Hello?

"Hey."

"What's up, lady? How are you doing?"

"I'm doing well. Have you thought about me?"

"What do you think?"

"You're right. You're right, but hey, I just wanted to let you know I appreciate you taking me out for dinner. I had a lovely time. It's been a while since I was able to relax and have a calm night without any distractions and any madness. It can be tough out here being an adult when you have multiple hustles to get to the bag."

Kofi agreed. "Yeah, tell me about it. And you don't have to thank me."

"I want you to have a drink with me. How about you come over?"

Kofi thought it was tempting. "I thought with me being married you were easily scared away."

"Funny. Can you come see me or not?" Selma didn't hold back.

Kofi looked back near the door of the office and put his hand over the phone, and he lowered his voice. He heard footsteps, but it was Liviana going to bathroom. He continued the conversation once he heard the bathroom door shut. "Where are you right now?"

"I'm at my condo. What's it gonna be? Or you need permission?"

"I'm a grown ass man."

"If you are, then come bring your grown ass over here." Selma challenged Kofi.

Liviana was Kofi's wallpaper on his phone, and he looked at it several times after he closed his laptop. She was on her way to bed. She was a heavy sleeper. Such a heavy sleeper that if a robber came in, she wouldn't know. Kofi changed his clothes and laid in the bed for about an hour to wait for Liviana to go to sleep. He dozed off himself a couple times. His phone was on silent, and he received a couple text messages from Selma. She was teasing him about being scared.

Liviana moved her body while she was sleeping, and it startled Kofi. He quickly put his phone away. She turned the opposite direction and put the covers over her body. He slowly and carefully made his way off the bed and walked quietly out of the bedroom door.

When walked out, he kept the door cracked. He turned his brightness down on his phone. He texted Selma back that he was coming over.

When Kofi arrived, Selma was on the balcony with a glass of wine. Selma went back to the kitchen and grabbed another glass out of the cabinet. When Kofi arrived, Selma let him.

"Welcome," she said.

"Thanks for inviting me."

"I bet your heart was racing, wasn't it?" Selma joked. "Come in."

Kofi walked in slowly. "The jokes never seem to stop with you."

"Come over here and enjoy the view with me."

Kofi knew the only time a woman wanted company in the middle of the night meant one thing, but he still played it cool because a percentage of him didn't know if Selma just did want company. He had no business over there either way.

"How about giving me a tour of your crib?"

Selma showed Kofi around.

"What do you drink? I didn't wanna give you a drink you didn't like."

"It depends on what you have. I like wine here and there, but it's not my go to."

Selma showed Kofi where the bar was at. "Go head and help yourself. I have plenty flavors over there. Don't be shy."

He poured himself a glass of Crown Royal Vanilla Whisky.

"That surprises me," said Selma.

"Why?"

"Didn't think that would be your style of taste. That's all," she replied.

"You shouldn't judge a book by its cover. I love all kinds of liquor, but I am an old soul at heart." They walked over to the window to see the water view. "I love this right here. Hell of a view." Kofi pointed outside with the glass of whisky in his hand. Selma's spot had a peaceful rooftop and had a hot tub. "Are you getting me drunk so you can seduce me?" asked Kofi in an obvious sarcastic manner.

"How about you just drink your drink and not assume anything?"

"Say that, then. You're right. Forgive me for assuming. Anyway, this place is perfect to lounge. A spot to just get away."

"Thank you, but it's only temporary. I'll only be here for like six months."

"Where do you plan on goin' after you leave here?"

"Why? Are you gonna follow my every move if I tell you?" Selma laughed. "I'm not exactly sure yet, but I want something bigger."

"I can understand that. My wife is in real estate, so maybe she can help you out whenever you're ready to make that move." Kofi had a lot of nerve.

"Your wife... Oh yeah, you are married, aren't you?" Selma was being sarcastic to see how Kofi's energy would change when poking at him, but he didn't budge. Selma turned around.

"Why did you say it like that?" he asked.

"Because... it takes balls for you to want to introduce another woman to your wife that you're clearly into, or it could just be plain stupidity. Maybe you have a death wish. How would that make you feel introducing me to your wife, knowing damn well you wanna do me? I see the way you look at me. I've noticed since the day I came into your job." Selma had a mouth on her.

"It could be a little bit of both, but I'm just helping you out by giving you a resource. It sounds like you gettin' ahead of yourself. You actin' like we've fucked before. Besides, my dick is a privilege."

"Look what time it is, and you snuck out of the house to come see me, so make it make sense to me, boo boo."

Kofi snickered. "I think I like where this is headed, but you're the one that sent me the invite. You clearly wanted me over here as much as I wanted to come over, so it's obvious you have your own motive. So, tell me what you want from me."

"You could've declined. At this present moment, I don't feel like talkin' about your wife. That's for damn sure. She doesn't mean shit to me. After all, I'm not married whatsoever."

Selma was serious. She turned her back on Kofi and took another drink. Kofi waited for the right time to slowly put his hands around Selma's waist. He took a couple quick glances at her body from head to toe. He touched her gently.

"Your hands might get you in trouble. Are you sure you wanna take this route with me?" asked Selma. Kofi ignored her. He didn't want to talk anymore. He wanted to talk with his body. While Kofi was behind Selma, she laughed quietly. He brushed his lips across the back of her neck and kissed it. She closed her eyes and let out a deep breath. "You crazy. Your body is so warm."

Kofi could've run away from the fornication but kept himself there. He wasn't willing to deny pleasure. At the moment, that wasn't the way he wanted to enjoy living.

"More like I'm willing and able Fuck crazy." Kofi's attractiveness was inviting. Selma melted the moment he embraced her. All rationality was distorted, and since the exchange, nothing was required of him. Kofi got the message that there was no commitment or relationship necessary.

The two went to Selma's bedroom. Kofi got on top of Selma after taking his clothes off. Kofi stared into Selma's eyes. His tongue became the life of the party. After receiving multiple orgasms from head, Selma was ready to be bent over to set the pace of what was about to go down. While being comfortable on Selma's bed, Kofi traced his index finger down Selma's long back tattoo where her hair cascading over it. He loved the tantalizing view of her hips and shoulders. While she arched, Selma looked over her shoulder where her eyes met with Kofi's. He moved in and out, slow, and fast. He went deep inside of Selma while giving her spanks to her ass, highlighting and accentuating the rhythms.

While in full control of his thrust and friction, Kofi turned his head to the side to watch Selma's breasts swaying in symphonic glory. Selma rocked back and forth, carnally fuckin' Kofi right back. Her upper body bounced, and Kofi made sure he didn't slip out. They both synced together perfectly when they came. Selma collapsed on her bed with her hair covering her face. She didn't expect Kofi to stay. Plus, she was too busy lost in a world of lust. He put his clothes back on and quietly saw himself out. He was being ignorantly blissful. He and Selma didn't know each other for too long, but he was attracted to her mysteriousness. The less he knew the better. There was nothing wrong with seducing the unknown and not wanting to know any history.

Kofi went to visit Afia. If he didn't see his mom in person, he would at least call several times a week to check on her. When he pulled up to her house, she was outside with a neighbor, who Kofi greeted as well. He kissed his mom on the cheek.

"Hi, son."

"Just coming through to make sure everything was good with you."

"I'm always fine, baby. Nothing to worry about with me. Getting older, but I'm still moving."

"I don't want to hear none of that old nonsense."

"How's Liviana? She doing well?"

"Yeah, for the most part. Outside of stressin' about her job. It's been up and down as of lately, but I'm always holdin' the fort down."

"When are you making me a grandmother?"

"Who knows. I don't have a set date to answer that for you, but what I can tell you is with everything goin' great at the clinic I'm thinkin' about doin' some traveling. You know? Expand and work on helpin' with medical conditions in different environments," he explained. "Not as far as internationally, but at least local traveling. You know some of these animals be too big to travel to a different office."

Afia thought that was a solid move. "Great. I'm sure that comes with a lot of patience."

Afia hit it right on the money.

"Exactly, but you know I've always been poised. I talked to a lot of people around the city who could use my analytical and communication skills to problem solve. I'd be a fool to turn that down." Kofi worked good under pressure. "I'm out, Mom. Just had to come tap in quick. And next time I come over here, I hope you have a man. I don't want you to be lonely."

Afia laughed. "As long as I have you, I'll never be alone."

Afia waved as Kofi pulled off.

It was Friday evening, and he wanted to have a night out with Jerrod. Jerrod was always with whatever. He made sure he was free. "Let's hit the Cabaret tonight. I'm ready to get lit!"

"Don't threaten me with a good time. You already know I'm down. When you tryna go? You want me to come scoop you?"

"Yeah, pull up on me. I say like around eleven. Matter fact, yo, I'll meet you there."

Kofi had five thousand on him. He usually didn't bring that much but tonight was different. Jerrod already arrived by the time Kofi got there. He got the champagne room for three hundred dollars. The atmosphere was intimate, and the women were of different ethnicities, friendly, and gorgeous from head to toe. They also provided the best hookah ambiance in the hood. The strip club life was no joke, and it could be wild. There were strippers inside that had no limits, either. They would let a man snort cocaine off their ass as long as the bread was right. A dancer that had a passion for their profession made a man spend more money.

Jerrod was handling the bottle service. He ordered Don Julio 1942 and Patron. Offthe rip, that was eight hundred dollars. He also got an order of lemon pepper wings. He tipped the bartender and lightly tapped one of her ass cheeks as she twerked once he asked her to. She blew him a kiss after she walked off.

Kofi had a natural charm. He attracted women because he stayed to himself, and he knew when and how to make eye contact at the right time to make a woman welt and fall to her knees. As he grabbed the bottle of Don Julio, he turned around and saw Selma. It caught him off guard when he saw her crawling around the stage before reaching the pole. She was a pro. She had one of the best stage presences in the whole club. Kofi put his drink down while watching Selma do a twisted ballerina move on the pole. She had some flexible ass hips with strong quad muscles. She followed up with a corkscrew spin. With her being busty, it was even more impressive that her breasts stayed in place. Her execution was flawlessly performed.

After she was done getting off the stage and picking up her money, she went to the back. Shortly after, she was conversing with other dancers.

"I'll be right back," said Kofi to Jerrod.

"Say no more, my nigga, but hurry up. We got all this ass on this table." Jerrod threw multiple hundreds in the air. Money was the motive, and it ruled everything. You had to pay to play.

Selma didn't see Kofi walking up behind her. He tapped her on her shoulder, and she turned.

"Kofi? What are you doing here?" Selma's body was oily and clean as always.

"I didn't know it was a crime to come check out the bar and have a good time," he replied sarcastically. "You were going crazy up there. Let me buy you a drink." Kofi ordered a mixed drink for Selma.

"Just 1 drink? No, no, baby. I need more than that." Selma was the type of woman that loved to be lit, and there were times she would drink herself on the edge of a blackout. Zero fucks were given when she was living her best life. The two tapped their glasses together. "Are you here by yourself?"

"I'm here with my man," he answered.

"Are you leaving anytime soon?"

"We basically just got here."

She whispered in Kofi's ear, "Let's go to the private room?"

Kofi was on board. "Yeah? What's back there?"

Selma rubbed her lips together. "Opportunity and a good time, baby."

Selma stroked Kofi's face in a sensual manner.

"It looks like I'll be taking you up on that offer. You lead the way, sexy," he replied, making Selma let out a stifled giggle.

The private room was more relaxed and comfortable. It was darkened, giving the room a mysterious glow. It had good back lighting as well. Kofi looked to see if there were any security cameras inside the room. He leaned in to try to get physical, but Selma stopped him. He was ready to take her panties off to get right to business. The purr of Selma's deep and raspy voice flipped a switch on him.

"Don't touch me," she said.

Kofi was confused. "What you mean? Why not?"

"You heard what I said. Only I can do the touching right now until I say you can. Do you understand me?" Selma wanted Kofi to fiend to touch her and to have his mouth salivating with temptation and naughty thoughts because he knew he couldn't.

Selma danced for him. She took her G-string off and bent over with her ass in his face so he was able to get a whiff of her wetness. He sat back while digging his fingers on the sofa. Kofi was thrilled for Selma to put on a performance, and she teased him.

"You're not making this any easier for me," he said.

She never took her eyes off Kofi. She looked back at him as her hair brushed across his face. He closed his eyes once those lovely breasts were in his face. He had no choice. She ground on his dick but didn't put all her weight on him.

"Got damn."

She placed her finger on his mouth and then placed her hands on his shoulder. While her breasts were forward, she slightly leaned back and moaned. She did a swat at his hands when she thought he was about to grab her. This was mental anguish, even though Kofi had the physical freedom to touch Selma whenever he pleased. He obeyed the rules until she told him to proceed. She had the perfect attitude and confidence. Kofi could feel Selma's oily skin when she grabbed his hand and put them on her stomach and ribs. He played around with her by acting like he was going to bite one of her nipples. She chuckled and clicked her tongue back at him. She turned away and backed off from him and slowly twerked, moving slow while she jiggled.

She gave him permission to touch her. She grabbed the back of his head and pushed his face between her big breasts that commanded attention from him. He gave her nipples a good tooth graze. When they were softly bitten, Selma felt an electrical shock through her body that sent chills down the back of her spine when Kofi dropped his finger in her ass. Kofi was rock hard and hungry. He wanted to eat Selma up before he fucked her into newly discovered heights. It was enough room for the two to maneuver.

"You have me acting unusual. I don't know what it is about you." It wasn't like the attention Kofi was receiving was out of the ordinary, and that was dating back since his teenage years. Selma had pussy power that would've made a strong man weak and a weak man brave. Kofi's mouth was starving. She straddled him while he continued to caress her nipples.

"Playtimes over!" Kofi was ready to give Selma a special prize.

Kofi picked Selma up passionately over his shoulder and dug his face into Selma's legs excitingly to bury himself in her juices. He formed his tongue into a taco position. Kofi loved being a munch. He kissed and tasted Selma like he was teleporting to the promise land while still being alive. Selma felt like she was being kissed by the Lord as Kofi's tongue fell into a pattern. Selma scratched the walls with her long nails while he had her legs remaining over his shoulders. She had the box that tasted like lemons that were dipped in thick ass syrup.

"Yes, eat it, baby. That's the spot," she said softly.

She trembled. Kofi slid his tongue up and down the seam of Selma's pussy lips and tickled her cervix. None of her juices were wasted. The eater and the eaten were sharing a special moment. Kofi was top tier when it came to fulfilling his destiny as a man. He was an expert driver at the wheel. Selma was ready to be fucked until they both laid in a puddle. He couldn't wait for his shaft to be given a warm wet hug from her.

Kofi calmly placed her down. Selma stood up and put one leg over Kofi's shoulder and placed her hand on the wall. She was comfortable and in a good position for Kofi's dick to dance around inside her womb. He teased the head of himself in and out. With his parameter, he could do any position he pleased. They switched positions, and he picked her up. While Kofi was stabbing Selma, they slipped and slid against each other, rocking back and forth. She bit his shoulders. Her body was celebrated and worshipped. It didn't take long for Kofi to unlock all her sweet spots. Selma grabbed Kofi's chin hair and pulled his face closer to her.

"This is where your home is," Selma said. "This is where the fuck your ass belongs at all times."

Those choice of words made Kofi go harder, but he took his time, even through excitement. Selma's labia minora gripped strongly around Kofi's shaft intensely. "Make me cum!" she screamed, and Kofi followed up with more thrusts and rolled his hips. "Cum with me! Faster! Deeper!"

Kofi was ahead of schedule, and Selma took off while he followed behind her. As soon as he came, Kofi went numb inside while her pussy still had a hold of him. She gave him a tickling ripple and plateaued. Selma still had plenty of moisture and touched every millimeter of his long dick. She bit his neck while her arms were wrapped around him. Kofi was panting while trying to catch his breath. Selma was calmed in sheer pleasure.

"You're a goddess," said Kofi while he put his clothes back on.

"Don't hype me," Selma replied.

"Shit, you're the one that's making my heart skip a beat. It's nothing like I felt before."

She fixed her hair before she grabbed Kofi's face again. "Your body was made for mine. You know just what to do to make it cooperate with yours."

"I feel you. You're the one that got a nigga all warm and cozy inside you... shit. That interior is luxurious, baby." Kofi looked at his phone. "Fuck. I gotta go. I know my man is probably wondering where the hell I'm at."

"Okay. I'll talk to you later. I gotta freshen up anyway and get back to work for the night. There's still paper to be made. The night is young." Selma put her panties back on but could still feel Kofi inside her. Their union was spiritual, and it was incomprehensible. Kofi thrived off secrecy, at least for the time being.

Jerrod saw Kofi walking back toward his direction. He stumbled before he sat down.

"Damn, nigga, where the fuck you been at? I was about to text you that I was about to dip out. Man, I'm telling you, bro. Sexy never goes out of style!"

"My bad. I had to make a call."

"Man, you ain't gotta lie to me, man."

Kofi was fast on his feet with his repones. Even though Jerrod was his best friend, he kept it to himself that Selma was stripper. "I just ordered a bottle of Ace of Spades, but it looks like you had enough to drink for the night."

Jerrod was worried about Kofi's intoxication level. "Nah, I'm about to have another shot right now. I'll know when it's time for me to stop drinking, nigga. *We* lit!"

More dancers came over and surrounded the

table. Kofi laughed at Jerrod getting motorboated, watching the glitter get on him. The club was closing in forty-five minutes. After just breaking off Selma, Kofi wanted to relax before he went home. In the back of his mind, he knew Liviana was gonna want some dick. When he was drunk, his performance level heightened.

"I'm about to roll out. I had enough of this shit for the night," said Kofi.

"Say less, bro. I'm rockin' out until they close. Hit me tomorrow," Jerrod replied. "And be careful too, nigga. Hopefully there ain't no checkpoints out for both of our sakes. We'll both be in booking."

Kofi entered the driveway, and he knew Liviana was still up but was hoping there was a chance she crashed. He tried his best to sober up. To protect himself, he had a plan to go straight to sleep, but he knew how Liviana operated when she was in her freak bag.

Upon entering his home, Kofi yawned and rubbed his face as Liviana came down the steps. His body was warm. "Damn, baby. How much did you have to drink tonight? And what took you so long? I'm not used to you staying out this late."

"Evidently too damn much, but I can function." Kofi took his shoes off and his jacket. He hung it up on the rack on the wall.

"You know what time it is. I've been waiting on you all night, baby." Kofi walked to the bedroom with Liviana was behind him. "I want him," Liviana said with authority while pointing near Koif's pants

"You want who?" Kofi already knew the answers. "

Don't play dumb with me, boy. Get your clothes off."

"Damn, can I get a shower first?"

Liviana was so demanding.

"Do you think I care about you getting a shower? No. I don't feel like waiting, I want it right now. Hurry up and drop those pants."

Kofi was wasted. He was supposed to be adamant on refreshing himself before being intimate with his wife. *Fuck it* he said to himself. He thought it would've been suspicious if he would've done so. Kofi got naked, and he laid on his back. Liviana was still in her bra and panties but got comfortable in between Kofi's legs. Before she started, Liviana made sure her body was relaxed, and she calmed her jaw. With excitement, Kofi already showed precum forming before Liviana got started. Liviana nuzzled her face and put Kofi inside her mouth. She sucked Kofi passionately as he rested his hands on her shoulders. Kofi's dick felt like a water balloon inside her mouth. She drooled like a baby. It was thrilling the way Liviana made her slurping sounds and talked when she had to catch her breathe. Kofi was in love with the spit bubbles and the whimpering. It felt incredible. Liviana massaged her hands around Kofi's abs to feel his smooth dolphin like skin.

Liviana was overfilled with stiffed meat, and she knew Kofi was ready to unload at any given time. Liviana noticed a familiar fruity taste on him. While she still was eating, the taste was unique to her. She thought she was trippin', but she kept going. She ran her mouth down the sides with a mischievous grin that struck her attention, and it made her eyebrows raise. Kofi didn't smell like he usually smelled down there. Liviana didn't want to stop in the middle of pleasuring her husband, but for a moment, she paused in her tracks and sniffed.

"Damn, baby. Why you stopping? Keep going. I never told you to stop."

"You got it, daddy. I'm sorry." Liviana bowed back down and remained on her knees while Kofi stood up to show his dominance over her. Liviana continued, but she couldn't get the scent and taste from out of her head.

He could slowly feel his soul being extracted. Kofi filled Liviana's mouth like a creamy donut. She swished around his life energy.

"Wow, baby. Look at you. That's my girl."

Liviana was still on her knees. Kofi gave her a couple head rubs and smacked her ass. Kofi talked to her as if she was slave, but she loved the affirmation that was mixed with humiliation. The couple had their own dynamic and happy buttons. She was an object when necessary. Liviana got up after she put her husband to sleep. He moved up to the top of the bed to get inside the covers. He was passed out. Liviana was observant. She gazed at him, and she rubbed her chin, thinking about where that scent was from. She thought Kofi could've very well penetrated pussy tonight before coming home to her.

It was Monday morning. Kofi poured himself some coffee after he finished getting ready for work. Liviana was in the bathroom applying her makeup.

She didn't have to overdress when she was at work, but she knew how to put it together. She put on a white editor blazer and a pair of heels. She walked out in the kitchen. Her body was smelling like Chanel. Kofi touched her ass and rubbed the fabric, examining the design of her outfit.

"Damn, Mrs. Dixon. That's what I love. Turn around and let me see you model for me."

"You're so silly," she replied bashfully.

"You on your way to make me some money?"

"You mean make us money? Say it right," replied Liviana.

"Say that, baby. Heard you!"

Kofi finally had his mobile truck clinic set up. He went outside and started the truck. He had every-thing he needed from digital scales, a portable X-Ray machine, his blood pressure monitor, and the centrifuge for liquid samples. He had several USB memory sticks that he'd store an animal's medical records in. Also, in the event that radiographs needed to be submitted for certain evaluations, he kept more than one. He stored his equipment inside his travel bag. He was leaving before Liviana. Kofi kissed Liviana.

"I'll see you later, baby."

When Kofi left out for work, he didn't realize he

dropped one of his USB memory sticks. When she picked up the USB drive. Liviana went in the bedroom and opened her laptop and stuck the drive inside the port. The USB popped up on the desktop, and she clicked on it. There was a folder that said exclusive content. *What the hell?* At first, Liviana took her fingers off the mouse, and she was unsure if she could click, but there was a voice in her head that was telling her to do so. When she clicked, there was a video of Kofi and a woman. At first, the woman wasn't visible enough for Liviana to see exactly who it was. She focused on the screen closer. There was a tattoo that was on the woman's lower back that looked familiar. Low and behold, Selma was the one in the video.

Liviana felt like her soul was about to fly out of her mouth from being speechless and slightly frightened by the images of watching her husband and Selma. When Liviana put it together that she and Kofi were both fuckin' Selma, not only was she in shock, but she knew she and Kofi were both pieces of shit. This was about to turn into Hiroshima. That dynamic was insane. They were both doing each other dirty.

At that point, she didn't know what to do or how to confront the situation. They both had an even score. One thing for certain, Liviana wasn't gonna keep it to herself for too long. She had to come up with a plan to reveal it out in the open. What was evident was the fact that there was about to be no such thing as discretion.

Chapter Twelve
A Fool's Game

Liviana had about an hour of free time before having an open house. There were several folks that were bidding on it. She wanted to make sure everything was solid before anybody came, but she also had other plans. At the time, she didn't know another environment to lure Selma and Kofi in, so she decided to have them both come to same location. Though it was a reckless move to choose, in her mind, she felt that sort of campaign was justified and strategic. She still couldn't believe she and her husband were both sleeping with the same woman. She took a drink of water, and she looked out the window of the house. After moving from the window, she walked outside in the yard. She decided she was calling Kofi first.

"Babe, I have something to show you," said Liviana.

"What's that?" asked Kofi.

"I want you to come over to my open house. I'm super excited. This house is so beautiful. Can you come over, please? You're gonna love this antique furniture and these royal designs in the house."

"Okay, I'm on my way. Just send me the location."

Liviana was already ahead of him. While she had him on speakerphone, the address was already sent to him. "The door will be unlocked when you get here. I'll be inside the house."

When Kofi told Liviana he was on his way, she wanted to know what Selma was doing, so she could invite her over as well. Liviana had Selma eating out the palm of her hands so she knew even if she was busy, she would still find a way over to see Liviana.

Kofi knocked on the door, and Liviana let him in.

"Damn, baby, you weren't lying. This house is fire."

"I know, right?"

"What else did you want to show me?"

The doorbell rang. Kofi stood near the marble countertop.

"Hold on, babe. I'll be right back. I'm going to answer that."

"I didn't know you had other company coming over. I thought it was just me," said Kofi.

Liviana ignored Kofi. Selma was at the door, and she greeted Liviana with a hug. Selma leaned in for a kiss, but Liviana backed up because she was in a professional setting, and she wanted it to be set up as her husband and Liviana were nothing but two business associates.

"Not right now, love," she whispered.

When Selma pulled up, she didn't notice Kofi's car. She completely overlooked it. If she would've seen it, she would've known something was up right away. Kofi's back was turned. He was on his phone, waiting for Liviana to come back from answering the door. He turned around at the same time Selma walked up. They saw each other at the same time, and instantly became befuddled. Kofi furrowed his eyebrows.

"What the fuck?"

All three of them were having a standoff with different facial expressions. Kofi and Selma looked petrified. Liviana gladly brought it to the surface.

"Since we're all here... we might as well get right to it."

"What the fuck is goin' on? And how do you two know each other?" Selma looked back and forth between Kofi and Liviana. "Can somebody answer me, please? What is this? Wait...You two are married? Kofi, is Liviana who you're married to?"

Liviana wasn't going to cause a big ass scene. Kofi stammered over his words. "See, I know... this isn't... Okay... look."

"Hold on a minute," Liviana said to Selma. "I know you're thrown off right now. I'll bring you up to speed. Yes, Kofi is my husband." For a moment, Selma barely knew what was happening, and she had uncontrollable blinks as she tilted her head. "I just want you to know I know you're cheating on me, baby," said Liviana. Kofi looked like a deer in the headlights. "But it's fine, baby, because I've been cheating on you as well... with her."

There was no way possible at that moment that either one of them could retain their dignity. That was the last thing Kofi was ready to hear. "Wait... Excuse me? You're doing what? Huh? What are you—"

Liviana hit Kofi with classic psychological projection. "I believe you heard what I just said."

Selma stood there in disbelief while Kofi's mind devolved into chaos. The tension was thick.

"How do you and Selma know each other?" asked Kofi.

Liviana had Kofi's flash drive in her hand and took it out of her pocket. "I think you dropped this," she replied as she tossed Kofi's flash drive, and he caught it with one hand.

"Shit," he mumbled.

"The movie is amazing, by the way. You're a great actor when the camera is on."

Kofi was about to do damage control. "You went through my stuff? That's how we gettin' down now, Liv?"

"No, no, no, no, don't even try that trick shit with me. You're asking the wrong questions. That's not relevant right now, honey, because we have a bigger problem."

The couple had a decision to make. Selma was caught in the middle.

"I think I need to go," suggested Selma. "I don't want to get involved in this. This is weird. This doesn't have anything to do with me. I don't know what this is, but I damn sure ain't staying for it."

"You're already involved. It's too late for that. You have everything to do with it," said Liviana.

Selma didn't have time for the bullshit. "Yeah... well... either way, I'm not staying here for it. I'll kindly see myself out. This is a nice house, by the way."

Liviana didn't bother trying to keep Selma there. She walked out, and there was an awkward silence in the house. Kofi tapped his fingers on the counter and he could feel Liviana staring in his direction.

"Nothing to say?" Kofi and Liviana had a shortfall between the two of them. Liviana went outside, leaving Kofi in the kitchen by himself. She called to cancel her open house, because she knew she wasn't willing to focus on her business for the rest of the day. Their marriage was deteriorating.

Later that night, Kofi came in the bedroom where Liviana was watching TV on the bed. She was getting tired, but she sat up when he sat right next to her. He turned the TV off.

"We have a lot of talkin' to do, woman."

Liviana agreed as she yawned. "I agree, but I just don't know where to begin."

"What are we supposed to do? Do you care about her? Do you have feelings for her? There must be a solution to this, and it better be sooner than later."

The couple's actions spiraled out of control, and they both had to come up with a decision on whether they were going to keep their marriage. It wasn't about their relationship needing to be saved. "Why did this even happen? I mean, it's not like we can place blame on her. Looks like we both have fucked up errors in our ways."

Kofi was always a player, but Liviana's personality didn't mesh with her actions, so Kofi was surprised, and his pride was crushed by it, even though he didn't want to admit it. Kofi was thinking if it was possible to have a common ground potentially.

"Since when do you like women?"

"I don't know. I guess I was feeling alone. You weren't paying attention to me like I kept stressin' to you, but you wouldn't listen. Me and Selma just clicked, and one thing led to another. We were around each other a lot. We hung out. The night we had a girl's night, I experimented. Things happened so quickly. I didn't even think I was into women, but she made me feel so comfortable and free. In a way it, was an escape. To be real, I don't even know who I am anymore. I'm out of my character, and I'm confused."

Kofi didn't know what to do or say about what Liviana just shared. "I'm drawing a blank. Is our marriage fixable?"

"I want you to tell me it's going to stop from here on out. We put a lot in this marriage. We love each other. We're trying to build an empire. We're better off together than apart."

Kofi looked at Liviana. He couldn't believe how well she was taking the situation. "Can we promise each other we don't hurt each other anymore?"

Liviana was willing to rebuild their relationship if there even was a possibility of reconciliation. It most likely would be a long road to recovery. Liviana was goin' through an identity crisis, but she was willing to save her marriage, even if that meant to go to the ends of the earth to do so.

"Do you think it's that simple? Like things can go back to normal? I find it hard to believe there won't be some type of resentment in the center of this shit."

"Why are you doubting it?"

"I don't know... maybe because we both been fuckin' the same woman. It's not exactly something that can just *poof!* Be erased out the memory bank.

Plus, you being as nonchalant the way you are is scaring the shit out of me. I know how women are. They say they're over something, and they're not. They let shit linger long as shit, and it bottles up before they implode," he explained. "Did you forget how much I know women?"

"I'm not in the mood for your cocky ass bullshit. Give me your word that this ends now. I was doing what I was doing for all the wrong reasons. I let her in my head, and she was so friendly and sweet to me. Did I enjoy it for the moment? Yes, I can't lie about that, but it's not the woman I wanna continue to be. I realized that right away. I'm not in the business of wanting to cause more damage to myself. I'll call her later to let her know I can't see her anymore, and this is over," said Liviana.

In the back of Kofi's mind, he was reluctant of stopping his behavior. He got a rush from a woman being an accomplice to his dirty activities, and he also believed it wouldn't have mattered if he broke it off with Selma. He was in too deep, and she would just undermine it. This was an obligation that Liviana was enforcing.

"Promise me, Kofi, that you're gonna cut off contact from her."

"Okay, I promise," Kofi said quickly.

Liviana didn't feel it was genuine, but she decided to give him the benefit of the doubt, even though she didn't like the facial expression he presented because it looked like he was just trying to shut her ass up. He needed a distraction to clear his head, so he decided to head to the gym. "I'ma go workout."

"You sure that's where you're going?"

"Let me guess, you're gonna start clockin' me? Next thing I know, you're gonna be wanting me to drop my location every time I leave the house."

Liviana didn't want to argue. She knew Kofi going to the gym was a regular routine and not out of the ordinary. "Whatever you say. Just go. I'll see you later. Go have fun."

Afia was coming from a date. She was over at his house, and he cooked her dinner. She was on her way home when Kofi called her because he wanted to vent. When she got home, Kofi was already at the house waiting for her. When she saw her son's face,

Afia could sense something was off. She took her stuff off and sat next to Kofi on the couch.

"Talk, to me, baby. What's wrong?"

"I wanted your opinion on something I was thinking about," Kofi replied. "Why do you think I got married too fast?"

Afia wanted to keep her opinion to herself at first. "You love Liviana right?"

"Of course, I do."

"Then it doesn't matter, son. Plus, you're already married and happily married at that."

"It matters to me. I guess it depends on the definition of happily. Lately, I've been feeling like I forced this."

"I'm not liking the sound of that. I do believe you jumped into marriage fast, but a boy to a man, you're supposed to figure out your way in life and move accordingly by standing on what your decisions. You and Liviana were supposed to be on the same page on your motivations inside the marriage. You followed your heart," Afia explained. "Whether it be who you decide to be with, I've always felt that love wasn't just a feeling, but it's a lifetime commitment to where you're putting your needs to the side to dedicate yourself to your lover. Liviana is a sweet woman, and she loves you. Now sure, there's worse days than others that will test your faith. You must decide whether that person is worth it or not. Inner peace means everything. Whatever the hump is between you two, because it's none of my business, I have faith you'll recover. I don't mean to go off on a tangent if I am. You two make a perfect pair. Don't lose sight of that. That's all I'll say."

Afia couldn't hold Kofi's hand anymore. His decisions were his decisions. She had an idea of what might've been going on, but she minded her business. Afia wished Kofi and Liviana had more realistic talks before adding such an important and serious situation like marriage into the equation.

"Where I'm at right now is something that's unavoidable. I don't know what to do about it. I feel like she knows we've been growing apart. She isn't the same woman from when we were still teenagers, rightfully so. I know people change. Our bodies change, and even with kids, that means that intimacy changes. It's not my fault. It's just how it is. I didn't make the rules up."

"Nothing can stop you if you and Liviana both stay committed to each other."

Kofi thought deeply about his mother's words.

Liviana went over to Selma's house to talk about the incident that happened at the open house. It wasn't gonna be easy to talk about the elephant in the room, but she was willing to be a woman about the situation. She let her right in.

"Thanks for letting me come over. I just wanted to talk," Liviana said.

"No problem. What's up?"

"I know the other day was awkward, and I'm sorry for having to lure you and Kofi in the manner that I did. I don't blame you for leaving the way you did. It was childish of me, but we're in a mess right now. As you know, I know Kofi's been cheating on me with, you and I've been doing the same. Never in a million years did I ever think I'd violate myself like this."

Selma studied Liviana. "Mhm, go on."

"I say that to say I wanna continue to work on my marriage with Kofi. Me and you, of course, hit it off well, and you showed me a great time. It... was..."

"It was what?"

"I never did that before."

"You enjoyed it, though, didn't you?"

Selma didn't have to ask Liviana that because the proof was in the pudding.

"That's not important, but what rubbed me the wrong way was watchin' both of you on video. Can we just forget that any of this happened? Like we just can push this shit to the back of our minds and go on with our lives. Me and you started off as friends. I felt helpless and stressed out, and you bridged that gap for me, and you made me open up through your support. Considering the turn of events, I'm not sure it's possible if we can remain friends." Selma wasn't at all moved, but she understood. "Don't get me wrong, I don't at all feel guilty of my actions that night. You made me feel good, but this is wrong. You and Kofi can't talk anymore."

Liviana wasn't taking heed to the fact that confronting Selma about Kofi could've made matters worse, but she was respecting herself enough to walk away. She didn't want to be in a position where she would be fighting an outsider because this wasn't a competition to her. "He will remain my priority. As a woman, I'm coming to you to ask you if you will respect that?"

Selma smiled, but it was a fake one. "Sure."

"Thank you." She reached her hands out for a hug in which Selma obliged. "I don't want it to be weird if we run into each other, and we act like we don't exist."

"Absolutely. There's no love lost with me."

. "I guess there isn't anything else to say." Selma gave Liviana one more kiss on her lips before she left.

Selma was a great pretender at that moment. As much as she was being friendly and showed her understanding of where Liviana was coming from, she was still threatening the marriage subliminally. She had other plans up her sleeve. No sooner than Liviana left Selma's, she recieved a call from Kofi that they needed to talk. At this time, Selma was annoyed with everybody wanting to talk. She rolled her eyes when she looked at her phone but got over it. She didn't wanna be at her crib, so she met up with him at John D. Macarthur Beach State Park.

Upon arrival, she realized she was the only one on the beach as she stretched her feet across the sand. She turned around, and Kofi was behind her.

"We gotta end this..." said Kofi with a sense of doubt in his voice.

"That doesn't sound too convincing to me. You look unsure of yourself."

Kofi's eyes were looking at the sand. Selma took her shades off.

"Why can't you look at me when you say it?" She stood up. Kofi was fighting it. Selma played off it because she was aware of how much he was captivated by her. "Do you really wanna leave me alone?"

He stumbled over his words and grabbed Selma's arms. "This shit is reckless, but as much as its dangerous, I'm lovin' it."

"Explain to me why it's so hard."

"You already know why, Selma."

"It's fine. You don't have to say anything. I know you're confused. I know I at least opened your eyes. I know where you wanna be. Liviana doesn't have to have all the fun. We can make this work."

"Yeah, but how are we supposed to continue when you know I have a wife at home? This is just gasoline to fire already."

Selma was willing to take her chances. "Did you hear me tell you to leave her? No. I mean, all you need do is keep up with your husband duties at home so she's not suspecting shit. You don't want her to grow suspicious."

"Something is wrong with you. You're cold, but I'd be lying to myself if I said I didn't want you," said Kofi.

"Indeed, but it's all about me, baby. It's not hard. I love how you thought letting me go was that easy." Selma laughed, but Kofi didn't find her sarcasm humorous.

"It's time for me to go. I'll talk to you later." As Kofi was about to leave, Selma grabbed his arm and pulled him closer to her and tounged him down. He engaged in the tongue action and grabbed her cheeks firmly.

"Mmm... Come back soon. I'm not going anywhere."

Kofi was gonna drag this out for as long as he could but had to move accordingly. He walked off the beach, and Selma knew that her kitty was bomb.

When Kofi returned home, he found Liviana cleaning inside his office. It didn't alarm him. He cleared his throat, and it made her jump because she didn't hear him coming in the door.

"Don't do that again!" she hollered.

"I'm sorry, baby. I just couldn't resist. Let me guess, is cleaning gonna be on your schedule for the rest of the day? I know how you are when you get in your bag."

Sometimes Liviana didn't wanna be bothered

when she deep cleaned the house from top to bottom, and she hated being interrupted in the process.

"Where were you coming from?" asked Liviana.

"I had to make a run to go check something out."

"Oh yeah? Like what? I could've tagged along."

"Not something but someone."

Liviana turned around and put her dust rag to the side. "Who are you talkin' about?"

"It's over and done with," said Kofi.

"What is?"

"Between me and Selma. I cut that shit off." Kofi grabbed Liviana's hand and kissed it. Liviana didn't know that Kofi went to talk to Selma.

"That could've just been a text message. Why did you feel the need to see her face to face to tell her that?" That didn't sit well with her.

"Listen, I love you, and we need to keep that love between us. You don't have to worry about anything else. You'll get nothing but one hundred percent transparency with me. I'm all in. Do you believe me?"

Liviana didn't say anything at first as she looked Kofi in his eyes. "I believe you."

Kofi gripped her tightly when he hugged her. He didn't see Liviana's facial expression of doubt. She was in a losing proposition. Kofi was internally still contemplating his relationship with Selma. Liviana couldn't play it by ear by allowing herself to sit and wait to truly see a change and trust that Kofi wasn't reverting to Selma. Too many times she was frustrated, ashamed, and embarrassed with her marriage. After all, Kofi was all Liviana knew as far as meaningful relationships. Nobody wanted to feel deteriorated, nor did she want Kofi's behavior to dictate her moods.

Chapter Thirteen

Caution to The Wind

A month went by, and Liviana was meeting up with a private investigator that she discovered on a website, and it stated that she specialized infidelity cases. She had doubt that Kofi's promise of not talking to Selma wasn't genuine and that he was still being sneaky. He would grow irritated with her questioning his whereabouts constantly. They would argue over petty shit. She doubted his sincerity. There was the voice in her head that was telling her something remained in the air, which made her awareness heighten. She had a right to confront those suspicions.

Liviana sat on the bench. She waited for the private investigator to show up. She looked at her watch. A random voice from behind her called her name, and it startled her. It was the PI.

"Oh!" She jumped.

"Are you, Liviana Dixon?"

"Yes, that's me. Thank you for meeting me out here."

The private investigator reached her hand out to shake Liviana's. It was a woman by the name of Kate Newman. She was bulldog at her job. She was a trained professional at gathering information and surveillance. She was the real deal and hardcore. "I see that you think that your husband is having an affair. My agency notified me of the situation. Thank you for choosing me. Just know our company isn't cheap, so you have top of the line service."

"I think he's still cheating on me."

"What do you mean still?"

"That's a long ass story, but to make it short, we had a situation where I thought an issue was resolved, but something is telling me it's lingering behind my back, so I need you to find out for me."

Kate thought that what Liviana told her was vague. "Is there a possibility you could just be paranoid?"

Liviana folded her arms. "We had an understanding the first time when we went through shit. Maybe my thoughts are being misinterpreted, but in my gut I know I'm right about what I'm feeling. Any other questions? I just need your professional assistance with this matter, and your resume is impressive."

"Can you possibly get phone records? Are you both on the same phone account? Because if you are, you'll be able to get that information for me so I can look into if he's been in contact with this woman. It'll also be helpful if I knew the woman's name, and if you had a picture of her. I'll need her address as well. All the key elements.

Liviana affirmed that she could get her all that.

"Don't worry. I know the nature of a cheater, and I understand the feeling of intuition."

"How do I know he won't catch you spying?"

"He won't. Your husband won't even know I'm there. I'm never detected. Our identity is always protected. Nobody even knows what our cars look like."

Liviana was sold. "I need to see it to believe it. My husband and I don't have a history of crazy shit in our relationship besides one situation, and that has to do with what we're going through now.

There's a conflict I need resolved. I'm a visual woman. I hope for his case I'm imagining shit that isn't there. I want you to prove to me I'm wrong because I don't wanna be right."

Four days went by, and Newman didn't have any unusual footage of Kofi yet. Though Kofi never gave Liviana his cell phone passcode, nor his social media account passcodes, she found a burner phone on his side of the bed. When she picked it up and turned it on, there wasn't a passcode. She opened it, and there weren't any contacts inside it besides one number, which was used frequently. The number was stored under a man's name, and when she tapped the contact to see the number, she grabbed her phone to see if the number matched Selma's number. Low and behold... Kofi was desperate to try to mask Selma's identity. She headed straight to Selma's house.

Liviana knocked on Selma's door. When she opened the door, she only had a robe on. She looked through the peephole before opening the door, and she snickered when she saw who it was.

"Well, hey, stranger. Come on in. Something I can help you with?"

"I'm fine right where I'm at, thank you. Yes, there is," Liviana replied.

"Okay, what do I owe the pleasure?"

Liviana closed her hands together. "I thought I made it abundantly clear that there wasn't supposed to be anymore contact between not only us but with Kofi. I told you I wanted you to stop seeing my fuckin' husband, and you didn't listen."

At first, Selma tried to play it off as if she didn't know what Liviana was referring to. Liviana didn't bother to let Selma know she had the proof.

"The dealings me and you had been over with, but you still choose to partake in having relations with my husband. Get your own man. Why? You're a disrespectful bitch. No, better yet, a murdering bitch. You wanna know why? Because you wanna be a catalyst of damaging a relationship."

Liviana was pissed off. Selma couldn't believe what Liviana tried to pull. She placed her hand on her hip in confusion and was flabbergasted. "Fascinating perspective, my love. Looks like the marriage was already damaged as far as I'm concerned, sweetie. Don't put all the burden on me. And it's not my fault I filled that void of boredom in his life."

Liviana stepped closer. "Do you wanna repeat that for me? Say it again."

"Now you wanna be tough," Selma joked. "I mean, come on, Liviana... let's not act childish here. Both of you used me to a degree to get your frustrations out when you wanted to feel better about your marriage possibly tanking, right? I did both of you a favor. I allowed you to tantalize me, tease me, and have your way with me. I was the light in your eyes when Kofi wasn't paying attention to you." Selma sneered and touched Liviana's hair and brushed her cheek. "Whose fault is it that me and Kofi's emotions touched each other? What happened to both of you being under that contract? It seems to me like you both are in breach of it. So, tell me how I'm supposed to be showing any type of sympathy for you?"

Liviana scooted closer again. "I'm going to tell you this one last time. Back the fuck off my husband. I'm warning you, and this is the last one. We're not friends. You weren't who I thought you were. You're nobody. You're nothing," she whispered closely to Selma's face.

Selma puckered her lips to Liviana. "Is that a threat or a promise?"

"Call it what you want. Stay the fuck away from my man. This is your last warning. I tried to be nice." Liviana was living proof that hell hath no fury like a woman scorned because she was willing to go bat shit crazy over her husband

"Fair enough. Are we done here?"

Liviana walked away and stared Selma down before she turned away from her. Selma slammed the door shut. She went to the kitchen and made herself some breakfast, even though she wasn't the biggest breakfast eater, but it was a rare occasion.

After standing over the stove, she felt nauseous. She raced to the bathroom as her throat felt like there was lump in the back of it. She gagged when she finally reached the toilet and threw up. She caught her breath as she laid against the tub. Her throat was still acidic and throbbing, and she was miserable. She wondered if that was a sign but didn't want to jump to conclusions right away.

Liviana played it safe and didn't confront Kofi about knowing he was still dealing with Selma, but she wasn't gonna be surprised if she told Kofi that Liviana was aware. Liviana wanted it to look like she was stupid but continued like everything was normal. Selma wasn't heard from in a span of two weeks.

Kofi walked to his car scrolling through his phone before he looked up and saw Selma was out front and parked right next to him. "What the hell? Selma, what are you doing here?"

"No hi or I miss you?" she asked sarcastically.

"I mean, you just threw me off. I didn't expect you to be right here as soon as I got off." Kofi was agitated.

"Sorry I caught you off guard."

"What's up?"

A couple of Kofi's employees were clocking out for the day and waved at him as they drove off.

"I needed to talk to you and it's something that can't wait."

"Okay, so why didn't you call me or text me?"

"Because I thought it was better to talk to you in person about what I'm about to tell you."

Kofi didn't want to be kept in suspense. "What's it about? Tell me what it is. I hate suspense."

Selma subtly rubbed her belly, but Kofi didn't notice the sign she was giving off. "You're gonna be a daddy."

Selma just came out and said it. He had a blank stare on his face. Selma took her phone out and showed him the positive pregnancy test. Kofi looked at it and then walked around to the other side of the car.

"Fuck..." Kofi's face scrunched up, and Selma didn't like the look. She instantly got upset. "Are you serious?"

"What do you mean am I serious, Kofi? I literally just showed you the picture of the test."

He was in completely shock. "You just told me you were pregnant, and you told me at my place of business. What the fuck? Excuse if I can't think straight right now."

Selma scoffed. "Yeah, well, you need to hurry up and get your thoughts in order because the baby isn't going anywhere. And let's get this understood right away, this wasn't a conspiracy to hook you and reel you in to make your life fuckin' miserable. We both knew what we were doing this whole time, and shit happened. You know what happens when you're not using protection."

Kofi didn't know whether to be happy or sad

about having a child on the way and it not being with his wife. This was a game changer. Life was all good when he was maintaining his marriage and entertaining his side piece with no bullshit. A kid was changing all of that.

"Kofi, listen... you know I don't need shit from you. You know I get to my own bag. I'm independent, I take care of myself. This may not have been part of the plan, but I'm keepin' my baby. An abortion is out of the question if that was a thought in your mind."

"I don't know, Selma. I just don't know." Kofi scratched his head in frustration. "Why didn't you take morning after pills to prevent this shit?" Kofi leaned up against his car.

"What is there not to know? Are you afraid that I'll blow up your spot and that you won't be perfect to the public eye? Huh? You think I'll force you into getting a divorce from Liviana so I can have you to myself or say you can't see your child if you don't play by my rules?"

"Now that you mention it, it's creepin' in my mind now. How do I know it's even mine? And don't even get mad because that question holds weight. I don't know who else you might've been with." Kofi had to live with choosing his own self pleasure over his wife, who was transparent about what she expected of him, but he decided to go against the grain. He had to figure out the best way possible to tell Liviana, and that was risky because he could lose everything. His whole world felt like it was about to crumble because it was for certain he needed to be involved with Selma one way or another to a certain capacity. Kanye West's "Gold Digger" played in his head. *Got you for eighteen years.*

"Hmm... Now suddenly it matters to you on who else I was fuckin'?" Selma threw out air quotes. "I wasn't with anybody else besides you, and yeah, I knew you were married, and I played the game. Just know you both played with me. You know what's funny? And I know this may seem hypocritical of me to think I have any right to have any feelings in this matter, but did either of you think about me? And what do you expect me to say? If it makes you feel any better, we can stop all the extra shit between us since you're uncomfortable, and we can just focus on the future of our baby. Not only will I gladly take another test, but you can take a DNA test if you need proof that it's your baby. There's nothing to hide on my end, nigga."

Kofi had a decision to make on if he wanted to be around for the unfortunate events of the pregnancy and welcome his child into the world, all while being a selfish scumbag.

"I'm not forcing you to do anything." Selma had no shame with having a new way of life with a married man. She wasn't dumb, and in a sick way, she set out to prey upon him because she knew he couldn't get enough of her. She knew damn well she was enabling and assisting in emotionally harming Liviana, even though they were supposed to be friends. Liviana wasn't innocent by any means. She recognized fast where it was headed by stopping the engagement. Kofi was aware of what he bargained for.

"I just need a minute, Selma. Shit."

"Oh, you need a minute? This is gonna be a long road for me. I'll find out how far I am. I'll schedule it, and I'll let you know when it is. You're welcome to be a part of it." Selma didn't bother to tell Kofi about Liviana visiting her at her door.

"Once she finds out about this shit, I know she's moving on and taking me for everything I own. This marriage is about to be over! Fuck!"

Newman was across the street from the clinic

where she had eyes on Kofi and Selma and took more pictures.

"Gotcha," Newman whispered to herself. She made sure she was parked near a public establishment, so it wasn't illegal that she was also filming. Upon her doing that, she noticed it looked like a heated exchange between the two. Newman knew how to keep a low profile to prevent being compromised. When Newman zoomed in, her adrenaline was boosted, getting every angle. She documented all necessary activity. She saw Selma get closer to Kofi. Selma gave Kofi a kiss on the cheek.

"You'll be a great daddy. I don't want to fight. I'm too much a bad bitch to be acting ratchet. He or she will be beautiful. I'll give you the details of the first appointment. I won't bother you the rest of the day." Selma got in her car and drove off. Newman got the picture of Selma kissing Kofi.

Kofi had a clear schedule, so he linked up with Jerrod at his place. Jerrod was in his garage doing some rearranging. Kofi helped him put boxes away. After doing so, they wanted to roll up. They walked to Jerrod's car, where they both had their own blunts. Nobody was sharing blunts anymore because you never knew where a nigga's mouth was at.

"Man... I'm in a fucked up dilemma right now, bro. Fuck."

Jerrod just finished rolling his blunt before lighting it up. "How so? Wait, hold up, man. How come it seems like you always got some shit goin' on wit' you? Nigga, you're supposed to be living life with no bullshit. I need to start gettin' paid for every time you vent to me about some shit," Jerrod joked as he coughed and beat his chest.

"This one is deep. This will change everything." Kofi blew smoke out the window, and Jerrod noticed how worried Kofi's face looked.

"Lay it on me. Let me know what it is."

Kofi sighed before breakin' it down.

As soon as Jerrod heard the "P" word, he started coughing excessively. "Yo, are you serious? How the fuck did it get that deep? What does she do for a living?"

Kofi was ashamed when he lit up the blunt again. "That's not even half of it. She's a nail tech and a stripper. How about you explain to me how I'm thinkin' I'm the only one doin' fuck shit, and it turns out Liviana cheated on me, too. It turned out to be with the same chick I'm talkin' 'bout right now! How the fuck?"

Jerrod slowly turned his head toward Kofi. "A stripper? Yo, I knew you was nailin' one of them bitches at the strip club. That's who you got wit that one night we was out when you took hella long to get back?" Kofi stayed silent. "Yeah it was. You ain't even gotta confirm it. Unbelievable. After everything you just said, I need another blunt and something strong to drink. If that wasn't a DJ Clue bomb you just dropped on my ass just now, then I don't know what is. You fucked me up with that, man. I never would've thought of a triangle like that. It just goes to show that a stiff dick and a wet pussy don't have no brains. When do you plan on givin' the news to Liviana?"

Kofi didn't want Jerrod to remind him. He sucked his teeth. "Haven't thought about it yet. I just found out like three hours ago. I'm stressin' the fuck out. My luck ran out. You already know how many times we had the conversation about how hard it is being a man. Sometimes all that matters to us is that fulfillment, especially when a woman is in heat. Proceeding with caution gets thrown out the window when they're constantly throwing themselves at you. At that point, it's yours for the taking.

Isn't risking getting a chick pregnant half of the initial adventure?"

Jerrod was blown away by Kofi last question. "I mean, what is life without a lil' bit of stress in it? Furthermore, nigga, why you taggin' shit raw that ain't your wife? That's not like you. You're wildn'. Better get your head back in the game. Let me keep it a stack wit' you, don't play victim. We wrestle with our feelings all the time. That's always gonna happen. Granted, yeah, both of y'all did each other dirty, but you decided to keep the shit goin' the minute it was time to right the wrongs. This is your mess, bro, so now you need to find a way to clean the shit up, but most of all, and outside of that, you gotta step up to the plate for what it is you created. Shit ain't always rainbows and sunshine, and in your case, it's thunderstorms and tornadoes. Let her know."

Jerrod also went on to explain to Kofi that he needed to tread lightly because Liviana was a bright woman that picked up on vibes and funny energy.

Tuesday evening, Liviana was in Palm Bay conversing with a couple for a house, but the couple wasn't on the same page. Right in front of her the couple were arguing. The girlfriend was ready to buy, but the boyfriend was showing reluctance to the deal. Liviana was able to work him to agree. They respected Liviana's confidence.

After closing a deal with the couple, Liviana was on her way back to Miami. While on the highway, she got a call from Newman.

"Hello?"

"Hi, Mrs. Dixon. Are you available?"

"No, I'm not. I'm about two hours away, in route back home now."

"Okay. Once you get back home, let's talk. I have more details I need to share with you."

"What do you have for me?" Liviana was anxious.

Newman showed surveillance of Kofi and Selma at restaurants and hotels. The first time Liviana and Newman had their conversation, she didn't bother with the phone records but knew it was a good idea.

The last time she checked, Kofi only had one phone that was used for personal and business use. Liviana also had a GPS installed inside of Kofi's car, and he had no idea about it due to how well it was hidden. She constantly listened to her intuition. When she did her own investigation, she noticed Kofi was making more cash withdrawals instead of using his debit and credit cards. He was trying to protect his statements, which made sense. With how frequent he was visiting hotels with Selma, it lined up. Liviana's spine shot up after looking at the footage. She had enough.

After Newman gave Liviana the information, she was finally at the crossroads. She looked over the latest evidence. Kofi not only lied, but he wasn't the same man of pristine that he was in the beginning. Life wasn't the same. The past image of him blew away a long time ago. "

This man has made a mockery of me for far too damn long," she said calmly. Her eyes were open, but she wasn't there.

"Are you gonna be okay, ma'am?"

Liviana didn't answer her. She needed satisfaction, and her satisfaction was coming in the frame of getting even by fuckin' both Selma and Kofi's lives over the same way they did her. Liviana wanted to end it once and for all.

"I've finally concluded that my husband will remain absent from me physically and emotionally. I just need to face that fact," expressed Liviana to Newman. "But it's fine. It's just time to turn it up a notch."

Liviana was feeling massive vengeance. Newman didn't know how to take those words because they sounded cryptic.

"Don't you just love it when it's time for an asshole to get his comeuppance?" asked Liviana.

"Absolutely. Is all the documentation gonna be used in court? Because if it is, this'll give you so much leverage if you plan on divorcing him. You have a strategy, so that way, it'll be easy to get assets in order." Newman had four months worth of footage on Kofi's whereabouts.

"I'll keep you posted on that." Liviana needed a plan before taking action. "Thank you, Newman, for all your hard work. You did great job. Please, kindly show yourself out now."

Liviana paid Newman handsomely for her contributions.

"Understood. I'll keep in touch with you. When

you come up with a plan, I'll make sure everything is okay."

"Sounds good."

Liviana went to the gun and ammunition store. When she walked in, there were other customers looking at rifles, and she was greeted by the owner. He could tell it was her first time there as he looked at her window shopping. She walked over to the pistols, kneeling down and gazing at the different caliber of weapons. She put her hands on the glass.

"Do you need help with a specific gun, ma'am?" asked the owner.

"No. Right now, I'm just looking," she answered.

After looking at the guns, she pointed at the gun she wanted. The owner retrieved it and let her hold it. It had weight to it.

"Be careful."

"Sorry, this is my first time ever holding a gun. I never thought I would even consider buying a gun. I'm scared to shoot it." Liviana placed it back in the box and told the owner she was interested in getting it along with the appropriate box of bullets. He did a background check and recommended that she learn about gun safety and how to safely shoot her firearm. He was rather ecstatic to introduce her to shooting.

"Do you have some time to learn some important things?"

"Yes, I do. Just show me the way," she replied with eagerness.

After purchasing her firearm, she followed the owner to the shooting range.

"Keep in mind that your gun will always be loaded, and you should always know your target. Never have your finger on the trigger if you don't plan on shooting your target and destroying that motherfucker."

Liviana didn't expect the owner to say that with so much conviction, but she could tell he stood on business when it came to armory. She respected his emphasis, and she listened. He gave her eye and hearing protection. He showed her how to grip her gun, how to stand, and how to aim. He only put one bullet inside the chamber to start off. Liviana lifted it up and aimed at the target. Before she was about to pull the trigger, she relaxed her lungs. She pulled the trigger slowly and smoothly. She exhaled as she flinched.

"That was great!" hollered the owner.

She shot around for another hour, switching guns. She was excited that she found a new hobby, even though it was for the wrong reasons. She didn't show her excitement, but she used her anger as her motivator. Going overboard wasn't even a factor in her mind. She was good at hiding her poker face. Liviana was on a revenge mission, and she didn't give a fuck if her actions were counterproductive.

"Thank you for helping me, sir."

The demon inside Liviana was woken up the moment the gun was placed in her hand. It didn't take her long to shoot like a pro. She put her gun and her bullets in the bag and left the store.

Kofi and Selma made a grave mistake, and all Kofi had to do was level with Liviana, but instead, he tried his best to be a shitty ass nigga. The mending was over with.

The following night, Livian drove to Selma's condo. She was inside her car, and she was dressed in all black, and her hair was in a ponytail. She put her black hat on and exited her car slowly, but before doing so, inside the glove compartment was the gun she purchased. She grabbed it and put it inside her black hoodie. She went to the trunk and took out rope.

The ounce of control that Liviana once had was long gone. She slowly walked across the street to the location and looked around to make sure she blended in with the darkness. To her knowledge, there wasn't a person in sight that saw her. She was hoping she had luck of someone arriving to come in to let her inside so she could get to Selma's condo. She knew she was there because her car was there. She wanted to catch her by surprise, so she didn't wanna call Selma to let her up. When she saw a man approaching the door, she went out of sight for a second. She bent her brim of the hat to cover her face more. She jumped out fast and put the barrel of the gun to their lower back, making the person jump.

"Oh! Ahh!" the person yelled.

"Do as I say, and I won't pull this trigger. I'm not gonna hurt you. Just open the door and let me inside and haul your ass inside your home," she whispered quietly.

The person obeyed the orders, and Liviana forced her way inside. She made sure the person completely entered their home.

Liviana didn't think about the person calling the

cops, so she had to hurry to handle her business as quickly and swiftly as possible and get the fuck out. She was deranged. When she got to Selma's floor, the hallway was completely empty, and cameras couldn't spot her face. She was able to pick the lock. She noticed under the door it seemed dark inside. It was a good chance Selma was sleeping.

She successfully opened the door and crouched down. Bella was a heavy sleeper and didn't hear a peep. While entering the bedroom, there lied Selma slumped. Liviana stood there before attacking. She saw the lamp on the side and wanted Selma to know it was her. She turned the lamp on, and Selma slowly opened her eyes and tried to jump up fast. Liviana punched Selma in the face, damn near knocking her ass out cold. She grabbed the rope to put it around her neck and pulled as hard as she could.

Selma could feel her life slipping away from her. She was struggling to breathe. Her eyes watered from the blow to the nose, and it leaked. Her life slipped away. She had ligature marks on her neck. When Liviana got up from the bed, she looked to the left of Selma's bed and noticed a book that was sitting on the stand. When she looked closer at it, she saw there was a woman on the front that was holding her belly. The book was for first time moms. Once Liviana saw that, her fury went from boiling to complete fear, covering her mouth. She pulled the covers from Selma and saw her slight belly bump. She ran out of the condo before Bella started barking as she wept the whole way but keeping her face from showing as she pulled off and went home.

Liviana had no idea Selma was pregnant and was more furious that Kofi didn't tell her and kept it to himself. She committed murder and murdered an unborn child in the process.

Chapter Fourteen
Invisible Wounds

Liviana successfully got back home back by herself. She put her keys on the hook when she walked in. She lit candles in the living room, had a glass of wine, and sat in the dark while she put the fireplace on too. She looked at pictures on her phone of her and Kofi. She pulled a pack of cigarettes out of her pocket, which was totally out of her character. She felt like she was turning into a menace. Each day made her anger, pain, and confusion elevate.

Both Liviana and Kofi caused each other emotional soreness. Liviana's mental health was in disarray. Liviana put her head down and put her cigarette out. She could hear Kofi pulling up to the driveway. Her head remained down, and her leg shook from her anxiety. Kofi did the usual and sat in his car, but he eventually, opened the door.

He didn't realize Liviana was in the living room. He jumped and was startled. "Oh shit. I didn't even see you there." Liviana just stared and didn't say a word. Her faced looked evil. "What's going on? And why are you in the dark like this?"

"I wanted to talk to you." Liviana's body language was a huge tell. Awkward silence rose, and it was giving off ominous vibes. "I thought shit was gonna be different, Kofi." Liviana was crying. "The first time I met you, you showed me things I never saw before, which is why gravitated toward you in the beginning. I fought so much to not give you the time of the day back then when we were just teenagers, and you still a found a way to win my heart. I fell in love with you. It was supposed to be me and you against the world," explained Liviana. "The ball was dropped. It seemed like we were living on different sides of the spectrum. We stopped having faith in each other."

Kofi folded his arms. "The nerve of you. What about you, Liv? You have your skeletons, too. Am I the only one that did dirt? No! Let's stop pretending this was just my fault. We both knew what we were doing. We both were feeling like we weren't getting the attention we were supposed to be getting. It's like we were just used to each other and kept each other around just the pass the time," said Kofi honestly.

In retrospect, Liviana felt like their lives changed drastically after college, and even though they graduated college and got married, their lives were different when it came to goals.

"We made promises to God, and somewhere along the way, we both became compromised and sacrificed our ethics. We were supposed to be loyal to each other. We took each other's kindness for weakness, stabbing each other in the back so many times, we deceived each other. We copped out," he explained.

"I wish I could cut my losses and walk the fuck away. I wish I could mentally get rid of this nightmare and rip my brain out to forget about the damage you done. I've asked God to help, but it doesn't stop... the mental images won't leave!"

Kofi stood there stiff while listening. "Liviana, you need to calm down. You're not a victim. You were a volunteer, just like I was. I'm not the only one who cared about personal desires."

Kofi set Liviana off, and she walked into the kitchen and started throwing dishes at Kofi. Kofi ducked from a couple glasses hitting him, but one of the pieces struck him when the glass shattered against the wall. Kofi was cut on his cheek and had a small amount of blood.

"You see what you fuck you made me just do?" she hollered. She pointed at Kofi's face. "What makes you more of a piece of shit is that you had the audacity to relish in infidelity. You're just not a good person, even though you portray a certain image to people, but you're a joke." Kofi was trying to work his way closer to Liviana by slowly moving closer to her. "I've been abused, and the fucked up part about it is that as much pain you've inflicted on me, you can get away with it."

"Liviana, do you hear yourself?" asked Kofi. "You're not making sense. You are not a victim! Does it really matter who did who dirty first?"

"Feels like I'm drowning in quicksand," said Liviana.

Kofi didn't know where this was headed. "Excuse me?"

Liviana slowly pulled a revolver from her back, and it quickly alarmed Kofi.

"Yo! What the fuck are you doing, Liv?"

At that moment, it was rather poetic that Kofi found himself in the same position as his father. She slowly raised it and leveled it near Kofi's chest. Kofi's eyes grew so big they damn near popped out of his head. He put his hands up slowly and didn't make any sudden movements in fear of being shot.

"Baby, don't do this shit. We can work this shit out. I know this is a lot, but we can try to get through this. I'm aware of how deep this is. Just put the fuckin' gun down, please! I love you."

Liviana's facial muscles were tensed up viciously, and she was sobbing. "I can't! I wish I could, but I can't!"

"You're making a big ass mistake. I'm telling you, baby. We can rise and overcome. We can do counseling like you wanted to before. Killing me isn't the way. This is what you wanna do? End my life?" Kofi continued to plead.

"You drove me to do it," replied Liviana. "It just goes to show that you were never truly ready to be committed, just like your dad! Be real with yourself for once in your life. You can't convince me other-wise." Liviana wiped her eyes with the nose of the gun and pointed right back at Kofi. "It's too much to repair. I'm soulless. There's not much for you to say."

Kofi could see the pain in Liviana's eyes. She was ready to risk everything that was built.

"If you love me, then you wouldn't kill me. We've hurt each other. This is a two-way street, baby. There's plenty of times we were distant, and our infidelity lingered in the air, and we'd pull away. I'm holding myself accountable for my actions and been trying to figure out why I am the way I am. The question is, can you do it yourself?" asked Kofi. Kofi's heart felt like it was beating through his chest and was about to fall out. He was sweating his ass off, but he tried to compose himself the best way he could. Any given moment could've been the end of his life "Just put the gun down, Liv. It doesn't have to end like this. We can just move on!"

Liviana's hand were shaking. "You think it's that simple?"

"You can't come back for this if you make this decision. Think of everybody you're gonna hurt. My family, your family... come on now. Don't be irrational. I can't put myself in the same shoes as you," said Kofi.

"No, don't do that. You stole the most important

shit from me, and that's not only my sanity, but my time. That's something I can't get back. I had time to think about it, the only realization is that you're unremorseful."

Kofi was still pleading for his life, and he was getting desperate. All he wanted was a civil conversation to calm Liviana down, but it wasn't affective. "I'm standing here trying to make things right with you. I'm here. I'm with you, baby. Believe in me that we can weather this storm and move forward. No more lies, no more sneaking around... I'm your protector."

Liviana's mental was compromising her ability to act logical. "Funny that you say that, Kofi. Your M.O. is to do and say anything to get what you want at all costs, and I refuse to let you endanger me because you can't control your urges and be faithful. The best thing to do is protect myself, and a dead man can't cheat!"

Kofi closed his eyes and took a deep ass breath. He silently prayed to himself. He tried for the life of him to throw himself on Liviana's mercy, but it wasn't working. She knew he was desperate to try to reduce the pain so his life would be spared.

Liviana put her arm down. Kofi was surprised,

and Liviana walked closer to him. "I'm sorry. I don't know what's goin' on, or what I'm saying," said Liviana.

She walked toward Kofi and embraced him with a hug. He hugged her strongly. Liviana's left arm was around Kofi's waist. At that moment, Kofi totally blocked out the fact that Liviana was still toting the gun in her right hand. He thought the confrontation was over. Liviana raised the gun in the direction of Kofi and pressed it against his stomach while slowly gripping the trigger. "Liv! What are you—"

Liviana interrupted Kofi. "By the way, Selma is dead."

Liviana let off a single muffled gunshot to Kofi, and he immediately fell against the wall and slid down. Blood hit the wall. She jumped from the impact, surprising herself that she pulled the trigger. Kofi's muscles tensed up at a fast pace while holding his wound. He was in excruciating pain.

"Why?" he asked when he grunted in agony.

He looked at his stomach while clutching himself and looked at how much blood was on his hand. She stepped away from him, walking backward a few steps. It looked like she was spaced out.

Kofi struggled to pull his cell phone out of his pocket to call 911. He managed to grab his phone but wasn't fast enough before Liviana smacked it out of his hand. The phone was smeared with blood.

"Shit. Ugh..."

Hot blood poured from his mouth. His brain worked harder, and he was weak. Kofi took his last breaths but was desperately trying to hold on. Each second was harder to breathe, though. He put his hand out to Liviana while gasping for her.

"Liv..." Kofi talked slowly and was seeing the light at the end of the tunnel. He was having a beautiful dream before it was about to be over with. Liviana kneeled by Kofi's body. His brain was telling his lungs to let it go. His eyes closed, and he exhaled before it was all over.

Liviana got up and walked around the kitchen. She was immediately thought about what her fate was going to be. She couldn't believe she committed such a hateful and heinous murder of her husband. She came back to reality to understand that Kofi was dead. She was sure the neighbor gave complaints from the arguing and hearing the shot. Liviana was going down. She was mentally disturbed. She didn't foresee the consequences of her actions. She ran upstairs in the bedroom because she didn't have a lot of time. She grabbed a piece of notebook paper out of Kofi's office to write a letter goodbye as fast and as detailed as she could before the cops eventually showed up. Before writing, she could feel the toxic spit in the back of her throat, and she became nauseous. She ran to the bathroom and threw up from her internal struggle. She was torn to shreds ethereally, and she tried to tuck away her feeling of wanting to cry her heart out. Somehow she managed to before writing her letter.

MY DEVIANCE LETTER

Though this letter broke my heart to write, I would be dishonest if I wasn't in a desperate space. I was totally unaware of how much pain I was inflicting on not only myself but others. Yes, I was purely selfish, and my actions were out of piss poor recklessness. To say I was left with no choice would be bullshit, but this was my escape. I thought I was going to be with not only my lover but my

best friend for life, and he was going to
be forever committed to me. My love life
was no longer built off pure joy and
happiness but confusion and misery. I
did things out of my character. Now
I'm an empty shell. My inner thoughts
caused me to be destructive. I killed
Selma. I'm sorry, but I had to scorch
the earth. The mess was impossible to be
minimized.

To my family and other loved ones, I
know this was unbearable, and I left
you with unanswered questions, but just
know my life wasn't always like this.
Kofi was supposed to be my security. We
both failed each other, and now we're
here. This was the only decision in my
head that I felt would give me grace.
Maybe you'll understand, or maybe you
won't. This is a fucked up way for me
to be vulnerable, and I apologize for
letting you down and choosing the worst
way possible to navigate through my
problems. Unfortunately, this is classic

example of being desperate to feel better. I was the judge and the jury. Please forgive me. Kofi and I had to go. I felt that our souls found one another, but instead, I was sold a false reality. I wish I saw signs earlier of an immature sociopath. This was the best solution for a tranquil existence. Things turned out differently than I would've imagine, but when it's too damn dark, there is no light. Death is the only option. I just hope God can find a way to forgive me for the way I decided to carry on, and now I no longer feel numb and trapped. I don't have to twist in the wind anymore. The aberration ended tonight.

After the letter was finished, Liviana placed it on the dining room table. She looked out the window and saw a cop car drive into the parking lot. Two cops were at the door. She kissed Kofi's lifeless body for one last time.

One of the officers knocked on the door. They waited for a moment. The other officer rang the doorbell, and there was still no answer. Liviana made sure she wasn't seen when they used their flashlights to see through the window. She didn't want to be visible. Liviana's hand was shaking when she rose the gun against her head. The permanent state of sleep was more desperation than it was self-ish. She laid next to Kofi while having her finger rested lightly on the trigger. She put pressure on the grip and let it go.

The cops immediately grabbed their weapons when they heard the shot. They saw the flash of the gun.

"We have to go in there!" yelled one of the offi-cers. "Shots fired! Shots fired!" the officer radioed in, along with the location so there could be reinforce-ments. The cops kicked in the door and were greeted by the scene of Kofi and Liviana. They looked around the house for other victims, but it appeared off first arrival they were the only ones inside the house. They were stretched out the on floor. Blood was everywhere. One of the officers checked upstairs.

"It's clear!"

Once again, Detective Copeland was the one on the scene. He was smoking a cigarette before he flung it out in the middle of the street and blew smoke in the air. It was way for him to prepare himself for whatever he was about to see for each case he took on. He made his way under the yellow crime scene tape. He looked around the house and looked at the blood that surrounded the couple. Copeland was sharp on his feet. It didn't take him long to put the puzzle together while the medical examiner stood next to him.

The shell casings were picked up, and the gun was bagged up. "I'll never understand why things have to go this far. How do you sleep at night being a homicide detective and having to deal with this?"

Copeland ignored the officer because he was focused on the scene. "Not now."

Before the coroner was about to collect the bodies, Copeland stopped them in their tracks. "Wait just a minute," he ordered. He kneeled and was studying Kofi's face. "Where have I seen this gentleman before?" Copeland ended up having a flashback moment. The officers were concerned when they saw his face. "Oh... Jesus Christ," said Copeland.

"What's the problem, sir?"

"I know this victim, and I know his mom. I covered a similar case where her former husband was murdered and now her son." This was such a negative dynamic, and it came full circle fifteen years later.

Copeland excuses himself to run a background check on Kofi and Liviana. They got a positive identification. Ironically so, a woman pulled up to the scene with a CSI jacket on.

Copeland didn't know it was Afia that was pulling up to the scene. This was not only a dangerous circumstance, but it put him on high alert, and he had to explain this situation fast. Afia was getting out the car, nervously, as she recognized it was her son's house. She walked faster to the residence, and she saw Copeland. He tried stopping her in her tracks with his hands up to block her.

"Keith, what the fuck is going on here?"

He gently placed his hands on her arms. "Hey, hey, hey. We need to talk. I don't think it's a good idea for you to be here for this case."

Afia dropped her equipment. "What the fuck are you talking about? Why is my son's house police infested? Where is my son, Keith? Somebody better tell me something! Where the fuck is my son?" Afia bit her nails in suspense.

Copeland knew he had to inform Afia that Kofi was just killed. "He was shot."

Afia's whole world just collapsed in the matter of seconds. She yelped in emotional pain. "Not again!"

All Copeland could do was express his sympathy in the heat of the moment, even if it didn't mean much.

"You're a fuckin' liar!" Afia screamed as she tried to swing on Copeland. The officers had to restrain her before she tried to grab his weapon potentially. "Get your fuckin' hands off me! Now! Get off me! Where is my son?"

The officers were able to calm Afia down while she was hyperventilating. An ambulance was there and was about to put her on the oxygen tank. After brief difficulty, Copeland was able to receive additional information for other family members to come to the scene to be with Afia.

The following morning, Copeland got information from the medical examiner when he visited the office. It took time because the examiner had to recover the bullet and the path the bullet traveled.

The autopsy report came back that Liviana died from a self-inflicted gunshot wound to the head, and Kofi died from a single shot wound to the abdomen. Her toxicology report came back that she had Venalafaxine in her system, which helped with depression and anxiety. Copeland was told it could've contributed to her having suicidal thoughts.

Copeland knocked on Afia's door. Her brother answered. Afia was too broken to get up from the couch while she was being comforted. There was absolutely no way she was going to ever fathom losing her only son. Everybody was in the living room. At first, Copeland struggled to get words out.

"Hey, guys. I just wanted to go over some info, if you don't mind, or I can leave since this is clearly not a good time."

Afia was about to fall out, but she was caught and helped up by her brother. She was in agony. "I don't know how I'm going to adjust to the emptiness. How am can I continue to live? She took my only reason for living!" Afia didn't know how to trust life anymore. "Can you answer that for me, Keith? What am I supposed to do?"

"Listen, I'm not speaking to you as a detective, nor will I hit you with any stupid ass clichés, but I'm truly empathizing with you in this situation. I'm praying that God can give you strength to fight through this, Afia. She wanted to ease her own suffering. In a fucked up way, it's a way of controlling her own destiny. Whatever your son did in the past or the present time when he was married to Liviana, it didn't justify her actions. There already had to be some deep-rooted emotional instability beforehand that we're still investigating. That wasn't rational at all, no matter the violations he may have caused allegedly. Nobody is perfect."

Afia's head was down, and she slowly looked up at Copeland. "Thank you, Keith. My sincerest apologies for swinging on you last night."

"It's okay. There was a suicide note."

What did it say?" asked Afia. "Are you allowed to tell me the specifics inside of it?"

Copeland cleared his throat and sat down. "There were some infidelity issues involved apparently, and the recurrence to Liviana was too much to handle. Instead of the young lady having the courage to move on if she felt that problems were too much to repair, she decided to take both their lives."

Afia grabbed more tissues because more tears were flowing. "There's no such thing as life going back to normal for me. In a span of fifteen years, I've lost Lance and our son. I'm suffocating, and there's no shortcut to stop this." Afia felt she was gonna die from a broken heart. "My baby is gone!"

Afia was in a position where history repeated itself, ending up back where it started. Copeland was reluctant to break down what Liviana's suicide note said, but it was his duty to give the family some sort of clarity and form of closure.

"What I will say is affairs may have caused trauma, but it most certainly didn't have to end this way." Copeland got up from the couch and went toward the door. "There's no time stamp on grief. I know this'll be a long road. You know where to find me. Any of you can reach me at any time. Again, my condolences for this terrible loss. Afia, I'm sorry to have to put you through this again."

Before he was on his way out, Afia stopped him. "Thank you so much for your support, Keith."

"My pleasure. Take care, Afia."

Kofi and Liviana became proof that resentment, entitlement, and toxicity could kill love tremendously. They both were dishonest by walking a path of indolence, cruelty, and lust to make up for the suffocation they felt in different stages of their lives. Their entire worlds since young adults were wrapped around each other, which caused their love to dry up. They had great memories before the turmoil occurred. Their double lives were hiding behind closed doors.

Selma filled the void for Kofi, no matter how much he loved Liviana and tried to fight it. The bond became too deep, and she became a sheet anchor in his life.

Liviana and Selma's connection was purely based on temporary satisfaction. The fog surrounding the adventure made it uncanny. All parties broke a cardinal rule by thinking they could fulfill each other's needs. Liviana was held captive in her unstable emotions.

Everything didn't deserve happy endings, no matter how aroused you may get during a person's choice of ensembles. Love and hate coexisted, egos clashed, and the level of grief was unimaginable. Betrayal couldn't be justified, which Kofi and Liviana failed to take heed to, but the most important thing to remember was to never lose your sense of self and let love consume you due to someone exploiting your vulnerability. Anything could happen when you were blinded by rage. The tinted reality would leave you in deep anguish to overcome. Emotions weren't meant to be played with, and your first love wasn't perfect symmetry. Be prepared for the pendulum to swing back. Don't be trapped by your cravings, because chances were you wouldn't be able to untangle yourself.

The End.

CHECK OUT OTHER READS BY MICHAEL BASKERVILLE II

Trapped In Love with A Narcissist

Survival of the Trenches

Revelations: An erotic anecdote

Thorns of a Rose: Situationships of Poetry

Beautiful Scars: Free Spirits of Poetry

UP NEXT FROM STARLIT PUBLICATIONS

Queen Rae is hitting us with all new characters, but the same theme of first love next. Stay tuned!

Made in the USA
Middletown, DE
05 July 2023